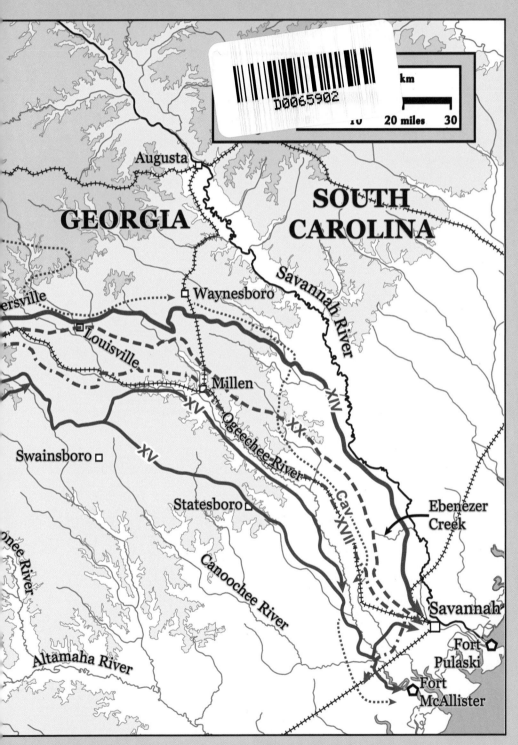

Augusta

GEORGIA

SOUTH
CAROLINA

Savannah River

Waynesboro

...ersville

Louisville

Millen

Swainsboro

XV

XV

Ogeechee River

XIV

XX

Cav.

XVII

Statesboro

Ebenezer
Creek

Canoochee River

...nee River

Altamaha River

Savannah

Fort
Pulaski

Fort
McAllister

km

20 miles   30

D0065902

The Ones They Left Behind

Antonio Elmaleh

21 CENT IMPRINTS

ISBN 978-0-9906406-2-2

Printed in the United States of America

First Printing: October 2014

ACKNOWLEDGEMENTS

I would like to thank the following institutions: The U.S. Army War College and its library at Carlisle Barracks, Carlisle, PA for access to and help with the unit histories of the Army of the Tennessee; The National Archives, Washington, D.C. for access to original Union Army service records; Duke University, whose library contains a significant collection of Confederate soldiers' letters and diaries; Robert Hemsley and The Detroit Institute of Art, home to the Winslow Homer painting on the book's cover, Defiance – Inviting a Shot Before Petersburg.

Much appreciation to the National Parks Service and its guides, who took me over hallowed ground from Shiloh to Bentonville, and made those places come alive with their knowledge and passion for preserving and honoring our legacy.

Many thanks to my friends Ed Elbert and Gail Steinbeck. I am grateful to my editors John Cusick and Winslow Eliot for their unerring thematic instincts and unflagging support for a first-time novelist. I would also like to thank Joe Marich/Marich Media (publicity, patient guidance); Donna Cohen (production, website design); Chandra Years (social media); Heather Parlato (book design), all of whose skills, experience and teamwork made it a pleasure to bring this book into the world.

I save my deepest gratitude to my wife and darling companion Anne. She is my true north.

And finally, my hat goes off to Gilbert Bates.

This book is inspired by a true story. In some instances,
people's names, unit locations and movements
during engagements have been changed.

*The emblem of the Fifteenth Corps, Army of the Tennessee, in which the Sixth Iowa Infantry served.

"We shall not cease from exploration
And the end of all our exploring
Will be to arrive where we started
And know the place for the first time...
And all shall be well and
All manner of thing shall be well
When the tongues of flame are in-folded
Into the knot of fire
And the fire and the rose are one."

"Little Gidding"
Thomas Stearns Eliot

PROLOGUE

Article in the New York World - June 5, 1917.

The Editors are proud to publish the remarks offered yesterday to the first graduating class of the Columbia University School of Journalism and to the recipients of the first Pulitzer Prizes by the Honorable Professor of Journalism Rufus Dewes:

"Graduating students, proud parents, distinguished colleagues and old friends. It is with pride and humility that I come here to speak at this commencement exercise. But first I cast a glance to heaven and echo my unshaking belief that the creator of this institution and these awards, Mr. Joseph Pulitzer, is smiling down from a unique vantage point in the great hereafter, knowing that the tradition he helped create and passionately upheld is alive and well in the hearts of the graduates and honorees whom I address today.

How inspiring it is that of our first four honorees for the prize bestowed in his name, three are women. They are receiving this award for the outstanding biography of an outstanding woman— their mother, Julia Ward Howe. Mrs. Howe has earned an honored place in our hearts and history for her lifelong work to elevate American women to equal status in our society—to have the right to vote and the right to earn equal pay for equal work.

But Mrs. Howe earned her place before that—for penning the words to a song, "the Battle Hymn of the Republic" that came to embody the national commitment to a purpose this country was founded on and for which hundreds of thousands of our brave Union men gave their lives in what some call 'The Great Rebellion', others prefer 'the War Between the States', but I say, 'the War Between Brothers'. Its impact and consequences will continue to shake the foundations of the Republic long after each of us here have joined Mr. Pulitzer.

My first story as a journalist is still the greatest story I have ever covered. That story started with a song as well. It was called "Marching Through Georgia". I was sixteen when I first heard it at a regimental reunion in Iowa in 1867. The story started with a wager and ended two thousand miles later. What, you may well ask, made this story so great in my eyes? Simply, how outstanding it was that one man went on a walk for national unity through the desolation of the post-war South and with all he met, down there and up here, discovered the better angels of their nature.

In 1867 we struggled to adjust to the loss of hundreds of thousands of men and to welcome home still more hundreds of thousands of wounded and scarred veterans. It was clear to me, listening to the endless war stories on the porch of Mr. Tompkins General Store, that although the shooting had stopped, this was not over. No one could agree about what to do with the states that had seceded from the Union. Some said we should put aside the painful anger we felt and bring them back into the Union. Others insisted that they be treated as vanquished foreigners, refugees barely existing in the hopelessness and destruction our armies had left behind, easy prey to carpetbagger schemes.

It was a war I did not get to fight. Being too young, I felt cheated of the chance to show I was as much a patriot as any of the veterans singing in that hall fifty years ago. All I had were questions. What were the lessons to be drawn from this War Between Brothers? Were we still brothers? And from such wholesale carnage, what kind of people did we aspire to be? My only resort was to live in books, diaries, maps, newspaper accounts, anything I could enmesh in my boundless imagination, so I might know what it was like to be there.

And then I went there.

I went on a journey with a man most thought crazy, others thought too damaged, but no one understood. And what I learned from him was that if we are to truly live as one nation, we would be wise to honor our obligation to walk in another man's shoes before passing judgment on his qualities as a man or nullifying his rights as a citizen.

Discovering this obligation for yourselves will grace your lives as journalists, biographers and historians. It will serve you better as people—to seek out and embrace the warm glow of a common good rather than to be exiled to the sharp, dark edges of division. If there is one lesson above all others from what we can all agree was Our War, surely it comes from scripture. 'A house divided against itself cannot stand'.

Go forth and develop with diligence and dedication the instincts you will need most but which will serve you best—to walk in another's shoes and to follow your stories wherever they lead. By serving those instincts, you must surely travel to a higher and better place than from whence you started.

Congratulations. Good luck. God speed."

CHAPTER I

The sweating, panting line of dusty men splashed across a stream that snaked through the golden red woods. Scurrying up the bank on the opposite side of the stream, they scrambled for a stone fence bordering a large field. Bare birches and yellowing maples flanked the field, which was covered with brittle corn stalks that poked out of the chilled ground like angry stakes. The exhausted Yankees collapsed behind the wall amidst a clattering of canteens, rifles and cartridge boxes.

The color bearer planted the unit's battle flag at the stone fence and flopped behind it, gasping for breath. He unhooked his musket and placed his cartridge box on the rocks before him. A colonel standing beside him swept the field through brass field glasses while his soldiers prepared for the fight.

"Just in time, boys," the colonel called out. "They're forming up."

The color bearer wiped the sweat from his eyes and peered over the stone fence. Bands of gray soldiers appeared like ghosts in the morning mist from the woods at the other end of the field about half a mile away. Tattered battle flags unfurled along the developing gray battle line.

A few white puffs rose into the air from the far edge of the field, echoed closely by the booming reports of Rebel artillery from the woods behind the gray battle line. The shells exploded well short of the Union line. A second volley sounded, this time landing closer. The exploding shells sent dirt, tree limbs and metal shards whizzing into the Union positions. Peering out between shell bursts, the color bearer saw shots puff out of Rebel rifles.

Too far away, he thought. Sure enough, bullets kicked up puffs of dirt a few yards short of the wall.

"Hold your fire, boys," the colonel said, staring through his field glasses. Suddenly he dropped the glasses. "Those crazy fools!"

The colonel's agonized outcry unsettled the color bearer. The colonel had led the regiment from the beginning and had always displayed complete calm under fire. What had upset him so much?

Minie balls whizzed by the color bearer's head as the Rebel lines came closer. Suddenly there was the distinctive, familiar crack of bullet on bone. The color bearer turned and saw the colonel blown off his feet. Blood flowered on the colonel's chest. The color bearer crawled over and cradled him in his arms. The colonel sighed, rolled his eyes up to heaven and died.

Another officer came to the color bearer's side, nodding gravely at the fallen colonel, and ducked as more shots hissed overhead. The officer arranged his tunic and belt. He caught the color bearer's gaze and looked back to the approaching Rebels. Dusting his lapels and squaring his shoulders, the officer drew his sword and barked orders.

The color bearer returned to the wall and peered over. Coming at him was a ragtag assortment of old men and young boys advancing across the field. An officer staggered ahead of the battle line, whirling his sword over his head and shouting drunken challenges to his men to keep advancing. The officer got tangled up in his scabbard and tripped as he turned front. Grandfathers and grandsons stepped around him and kept walking. The officer guffawed loudly, waving his sword and barking at the sky. Weaving as he rose, he staggered to catch up with his troops.

Now the gray line was but a hundred yards from the stone fence. Occasionally a Yankee got hit and tumbled across the wall. The Union veterans held their fire. They knew their colonel was down. Levering rounds into the chambers of their repeating rifles, they let the Rebels come, eyeballing the enemies' distance to their killing zone.

When the Rebels were close enough, the new commanding officer screamed, "Fire!"

The Yankees rose up as one and emptied a continuous sheet of well-aimed volleys into the gray line. Men and boys were blown backwards in windrows.

The color bearer had shot several Rebels and was fixing on another target when he hesitated. He was aiming at a boy of no more than thirteen. The boy stared back at him through the thickening smoke. His eyes glowed with the excitement of combat and the terror of death swirling around him. The boy clumsily reloaded and raised his rifle, which was almost as tall as he was, and aimed it at the color bearer. They both stared down their sights at each other. The color bearer lost sight of him when the two fired simultaneously and a cloud of black powder smoke engulfed them.

The only thing left was a ringing bell.

CHAPTER 2

The cowbell jarred him out of the dream he always had. Harriman
Hickenlooper sniffed, coughed and wiped his eyes. He pulled
on the straw hat that lay askew on his head and glanced at one of
his cows. On cue, she shook her head and clanged the bell again,
dragging him back to who and where he was.

"I know, I know," he muttered.

He rose, walked over to a shed, scooped out some feed and
dragged it over to a trough in a creaky wheelbarrow. "Come and
get it," he mumbled. The cow didn't move. "You wake me up 'cause
you're hungry, then you don't eat. Unh-unh." He pulled her toward
the trough. When she still resisted, he slapped her on the butt.
She lowed in complaint and moved to the trough. "There you go."
Looking up, he caught sight of someone approaching.

He could never get over the picture of Walter Ridley riding
a horse. There was a clear and mutual distrust between man and
animal that was obvious in the way Ridley shifted his weight in the
saddle to get comfortable, while at the same time trying to seem
composed. The horse just wanted him off. With opposite intentions,
they lurched down the road to Hickenlooper's farm.

Ridley waved a fleshy hand. "Good day, Harry."

"Harriman," he corrected.

Ridley was a big man with a small head. He had a baby's complexion, florid and shiny. His face showed of someone who wanted to reveal a secret, but was too proud to and hoped you'd notice. He offered a hand to Harriman. Harriman refused it, so Ridley wiped it on the pommel of his saddle. He scanned the farmstead.

"I worry about you, Harry. You're late on your payments again. And the place doesn't look so good. Are you all right?"

"Draw your own conclusions."

"Look, Harry, I am proud that the bank especially values its veterans. And I know it's been rough on you, with the war and your folks gone and all, but you've got to keep pulling. We all do."

Harriman raised his hand. "Spare me."

The gesture spooked the horse. Ridley grasped the reins. "Whoa! What's done is done. Let go of the past. Move on. All the boys have managed to. You have a nice home here. Your father and mother worked hard to make it that way. I hate to see one of my boys wasting his life, especially after all you've done for your country."

Harriman moved closer to Ridley. The horse shied back. "Did you come to remind me I'm late on payments, or to lecture me about making something of my life? Or to salute me for my service to my country? Or maybe because you're sorry for me. Which is it?"

Ridley shrugged. He was actually thinking all of the above, but adjusted his hat and tried to wheel his horse around. The animal didn't budge. "Well, no, Harry. I wanted to tell you about a regimental meeting a week from Thursday. Seven o'clock at the Town Hall. I hope you can make it. There's important things to discuss." Ridley clucked and jerked the stirrups. Nothing.

Harriman grabbed the horse by the reins and slapped its rump. The horse broke into a canter. Ridley's legs shot out of the stirrups.

Turning his attention to the fence by the road, Harriman was reminded of Uncle Reg. When Reg cracked that rare smile, his missing teeth stood out against a discolored row of pale white ones like the gaps where boards had fallen along the fence. It also reminded him of the holes in all the Georgia fences they'd pulled out for firewood.

Harriman's father, Owen Hickenlooper, had erected the fence once he had settled the farm outside Centerville in 1835. Homesteading—living and working on state-donated land—had drawn Owen and Molly Hickenlooper from western Maryland to the land rush triggered by Iowa's statehood in 1832. Making the farm work was tough from the get-go. Owen and Molly did it all themselves until the boys were old enough to pitch in. Things broke. Draft animals got sick, and worse, Owen or Molly did too, making one do the work of two.

There was never enough money. Harriman got his brother Alonzo's hand-me-down clothes when they fit him. He learned to sew his clothes, and anything else that needed it. What they ate came from what they grew and how much they got paid for it. Farm prices were unpredictable and could drop as suddenly as a September frost. Over time, the swings in crop prices and the savage Great Plains winters combined to draw the Hickenloopers further into an abyss of liens with Farmers and Mechanics Bank. Owen never showed the family the pressure he felt. He just went to bed later and got up earlier than everyone. Molly knew anyway.

It took Harriman all afternoon to fix one section of fence, with plenty more to do, but he smiled when he was done. "That's for Pop." He carried the tools and dead wood and stacked them next to the house where he'd been born. Was it twenty-two years ago? It didn't surprise him, and it didn't much bother him that he couldn't remember.

CHAPTER 3

Centerville, Iowa was founded in 1846, the same year the state was granted statehood, under the uncharacteristic name of Chaldea. It was changed to Senterville in honor of a Tennessee politician, William Tandy Senter. A clerk thought the name was misspelled and filed its incorporation papers as Centerville in 1855.

Slavery was a consistently controversial topic in the affairs of the nation. Iowa had been admitted into the Union under a compromise. It entered as a free state and Florida was admitted as a slave state in order to maintain the delicate balance that had defined national expansion from the beginning of the republic.

Centerville attracted waves of Nordic and Slavic immigrants fleeing religious and ethnic persecution in Europe. The rich, dark Iowa soil was a magnet to farmers who could soon boast that corn grew higher in Iowa than any other place on earth. Farming created a strong demand for equipment to harvest and transportation to move crops that newly chartered banks were eager to meet.

Harriman worked his wagon down the street, past Farmers and Mechanics Bank and the shops that supplied the town. It was the same covered wagon he'd ridden into town with his father and brother every Saturday morning since the boys were big enough to peer over the buckboards. Alonzo, being older, got to sit next to his father first while Harriman sat on the wagon bed and looked at the world backwards. Surprisingly, after his jealousy wore off—like all brothers, they fought a lot—he got to liking that view. Only occasionally would he crane his neck around to see what was coming. Often he'd just ask, "Are we there yet?" or "How much longer?" The view out the back made what was coming a surprise. The world appeared and disappeared behind him just as fast, but he had more time to see it.

Harriman pulled on the reins and stopped the wagon in front of Tompkins General Store. Several men sat talking on the porch, leaning their chairs against the side of the building. Some were missing an arm or a leg. As Harriman drew near, he heard snippets of their conversation; as usual, they were swapping war stories. Harriman hopped down, barely acknowledging them. Often their stories were exaggerated, fogged by opium, time, or the truth. They didn't vary much.

A dog wandered out of an adjacent alley. It bared its teeth at the sight of him. The hair on its mangy back raised like a hairy ridge. Harriman recoiled, eyeing it warily as he edged around it. The dog got pushed aside by someone leaving the store, giving Harriman his chance. He scooted inside. If people were amused by his standoff with the dog, he pretended not to see it. He thought he heard their whispers, the children tittering about the "man who gets spooked by a mangy old dog."

The door jingled and townsfolk turned to see who had entered. When they saw who it was, they turned back to their business, as though they felt sorry for him. Harriman moved along the counters, taking more than enough time to pick out what he needed. Several times, he picked something up, then changed his mind and put it back. When no one was looking, he slipped a bag of nails in his pocket. Old man Tompkins cast an eye toward Harriman as he attended to other people. Harriman scanned other goods, ignoring

Tompkins, hoping the storekeeper hadn't seen the lift. He waited for everyone to leave before approaching the counter, laid out his groceries and watched as the storekeeper toted up his bill.

"You didn't pay me last month, Harriman," Tompkins said without looking up.

"I know."

"This is very uncomfortable."

"I'm sorry."

"That's not good enough. It's not my business to keep extending you. If you need credit, see the bank. Walter was your commanding officer, for goodness sake. This is the last time. Don't make me cut you off."

"Please don't do that. Is there anything I can do, I mean, could you use a hand here?"

"What I could use is money. Your account is over one hundred dollars behind. Bring me some money or don't come back in here." Tompkins folded up Harriman's items smartly, then stared into the young man's face, betraying pity and disdain. He looked like he was about to say something else, but the door jingled open and a shopper entered. "No more of this, please," Tompkins whispered, then moved to the customer.

"I appreciate it," Harriman said over his shoulder. As he cleared the door, he snuck the bag of nails back in the bin and left. Looking around for the dog, he darted to his wagon and made his way out of town.

CHAPTER 4

They were Centerville's most prominent citizens—lawyers, doctors, an accountant, the Reverend Robus. They were gathered for the quarterly meeting of the Board of Directors of the Farmers and Mechanics Bank, Centerville's only bank. With little fanfare and short pleasantries, they were soon reviewing the quarter's results. Chairing the meeting was Walter Ridley.

"Generally, prices on wheat and corn have fallen, but our customers, with a few exceptions, have managed to stay current without much additional leverage on their accounts. I am seeing a few problems on the horizon. Actually, not just on the horizon, but right in front of us."

"Like what?" the Reverend asked out of concern for his flock.

"I am referring to the Hickenlooper farm. As you all may or may not know, Harriman Hickenlooper manages this property. Alone. To be frank, I have offered assistance numerous times, but he has steadfastly refused. Pride, I suppose."

"He was a good boy, wasn't he?" said Dr. Everts. "The Hickenloopers are—were—a good family."

"Is there anything we can do?" Reverend Sobus asked.

Ridley studied his hands, then the group for some moments. "I have thought of something, but it's highly unusual, and would need your approval, of course. It is not on the agenda." No one spoke, so Ridley took it as permission to proceed. "This life, this job, have treated me well. I have been blessed with the means to provide for my wife in a most comfortable fashion. We have not been blessed with children, but I consider our customers the next closest thing. I have earned enough also to contribute to my community, one I care about deeply. I have talked this matter over with Louise, and she wholeheartedly supports me. Should you, esteemed colleagues, give me your assent, I would like to purchase the note on the Hickenlooper farm from the bank."

"Why would you do that?" a director asked.

"His pride or feeble state of mind could lose him that farm. As his former commanding officer, as someone I led in the late war, as a fellow soldier, I won't let that happen. I'm sure all of you can understand that. I will stand behind him."

Heads nodded in support. Dr. Everts said, "You know I respect you, Walter, but my personal concern is whether you would put your fiduciary responsibility ahead of your loyalty to a fellow soldier, born of blood and smoke, and call his note should it be necessary. It could happen, you know. It could be awkward."

The committee members nodded solemnly.

"I have considered that. And of course I would do my duty. On the other hand, I trust everyone grasps the potential impact on our good standing if the bank foreclosed on a veteran. If it is just between him and me, it would protect the bank from any negative opinions in the matter." No one disagreed. "I will present something to this Board promptly, outlining on what terms I would relieve the bank of the obligation Mr. Hickenlooper currently has. I'm sure it will be deemed satisfactory. Agreed?" Again, no one objected. "Good. Then I will inform Harriman."

In fact, it didn't take anyone long to realize what an elegant way it was out of a touchy situation. A perennial problem loan on the books, with a possible messy ending, saved by a former commander personally standing behind one of his soldiers who was down on his luck. Good for the bank, good for the veteran, good for the community, and the right thing to do.

"Turning to our agenda, I would draw your attention to the latest year-end balance sheets I have drawn up. You will note that a month ahead of the close of this year, we are four percent ahead of our performance in the same period last year."

The discreet nodding of heads made Ridley smile.

CHAPTER 5

"I ain't dead yet," Red Hundley growled, watching the buzzards circle lazily in the sky above him. He spat a wad of brown tobacco juice, rearranged the red bandanna on his forehead and shifted his stringy body on the ground. He'd been lying in front of the abandoned shack for the better part of two hours.

It was from here that his wife and children had fled from the devil Sherman and his Yankee hordes as they were cutting a 60 mile-wide swath across Georgia on their March from Atlanta to the sea—a march that unleashed a tidal wave of refugees in all directions. These very buzzards had probably feasted on the thousands of horses and cows the Yankees killed rather than leave behind to the increasingly starved Confederate armies in the field.

Red stared into the crackling fire. The screech of a red-tailed hawk circling overhead disrupted the still air. Red-tails were his friends. He had sported their feathers in his cap all through the war, riding with Bedford Forrest's "shock cavalry" from Fort Donelson to Fort Pillow and a hundred fights in between. He would have ridden with "that devil Forrest," as Sherman called him, to the ends of the earth and had until the night he found out that "Cump" Sherman was making Georgia howl.

As the war dragged on into its fourth year, Red knew, as more and more of his fellow soldiers did as well, that their Cause was doomed. When he heard the news that Sherman was in Georgia, he did not hesitate. That very night, he and a few others packed the meager things they had and left. If he'd been caught, he would have been shot for desertion, but he never hesitated choosing between his family and his Cause. He never looked back. What he found when he came home was this abandoned shack and the ghosts of a family gone.

Lying there now, he could smell the cornbread and stew his wife always had waiting for him after a day working the fields. He could even see Delilah and Grace running up to greet him and smell their skin and their hair, redolent with lilac and straw. He swung them up over his head and gave them each a twirl, thrilled by their joyous squeals.

The largest buzzard shrieked overhead and swooped down, prompted by the shape waving his invisible daughters in the air. The buzzard landed some yards from him, waited, then hopped a few steps closer. More buzzards followed it down. The man watched from under the brim of his hat. For several moments, the birds watched and waited, hopping nearer, forming a feasting circle around the man. When the largest bird got within twenty feet of him, Red pulled a large Colt revolver from under his coat and fired. The buzzard's head disappeared, while the big bird's body hopped around for several seconds before it flopped to the ground. The other birds took off in a frenzy of beating wings and startled shrieks.

"I ain't dead yet," Red cackled. He cleaned his kill. Buzzard meat was edible fresh. And better than nothing at all.

CHAPTER 6

The Sixth Iowa Volunteer Infantry Regiment had been organized in Appanoose County. So it was to the county seat in Centerville that the farmers, lawyers, blacksmiths, clerks and schoolboys had come to muster into the 1st Division of the Fifteenth Corps, Army of the Tennessee, in July of 1861.

For four years the Sixth fought at Shiloh, Big Black River, Holly Springs, Missionary Ridge, Vicksburg, Kennesaw Mountain and the many battles around Atlanta. It took part in Sherman's March to the Sea through Georgia and up through the Carolinas to the climactic battle at Bentonville. It witnessed the surrender of the last standing Confederate army in Durham, North Carolina, six weeks after Appomattox. In all, it marched over two thousand miles during those four years of campaigning, and lost almost forty percent of its men.

For most men raised in small farm towns, the years of marching, fighting and dying across the Southland had been, and always would be, the most definitive experience of their lives. Regimental reunions carried special meaning, for they connected men to the memory of lost comrades while reaffirming a mutual commitment to each other now. These reunions gave the men a chance to sing "Marching

Through Georgia," a song commemorating Sherman's March; a chance to salute their battle flags, riddled with holes that mirrored the holes left in the fabric of their community; and a chance to tell their stories. It was a time for them to share a hope of building on their sacrifices and striving to make the lives they came home to better than the ones they left behind.

Bobbing lanterns lit the downtown darkness like fireflies, casting herky-jerk shadows across Centerville's Town Hall. Each firefly belonged to a surviving member of the Sixth Iowa. Some men strode easily, others hobbled on crutches, and still others rolled along in wheelchairs, pushed by their wives and stalked by memories of four years of war.

Walter Ridley rose to address the Sixth.

"Boys, welcome and thank you for coming out tonight. There's much to talk about. I have news about another shipment of prosthetic devices. New work opportunities have been brought to my attention. I invite those of you trying to locate your missing loved ones to keep writing the War Department with your requests. I have been in touch with the War Department, and they have assured me they are doing everything possible to connect families with their fallen."

Everyone knew of soldiers still listed as missing—hopefully buried, usually hastily, often in unmarked mass graves. The gnawing uncertainty about the fate of a soldier was still better than the pain and shame of those enduring a soldier's desertion, an act so ignominious that a deserter's family could never live it down. A few families had already moved out of Iowa rather than face the unspoken judgments and pregnant stares of the community.

The armies were always on the move during campaigning, making it impossible to bury every soldier individually after a fight. Often the army would return over the same ground it fought on previously while pursuing or retreating from the enemy. When they did, they often saw the skulls and bones of their comrades protruding from the earth, dug up by animals or denuded by erosion. What made it harder was that a soldier's unwritten code said not to leave your friends behind without putting them to rest properly. And yet they had to, more times than they cared to remember. War didn't wait for the dead.

Ridley was quiet and ran his stubby fingers over the names of the regiment's battles sewn into one of the battle flags behind him. He paused, bowing his head, then looked back at the now-silent audience. "What are we missing in our town?"

"A better mayor!" someone shouted.

Someone seconded him.

"You, Colonel!"

Ridley smiled broadly, but shook his head. "Think about it. We are missing a place where we may come, day or night, to honor those we left behind in the service of our noble Cause. What we're missing in Centerville is a place to honor the Sixth Volunteer Iowa Infantry."

"You talking a monument? That'd be nice," someone said. "But with all due respect, Colonel, I can't afford no memorial." The man gestured to his two little boys with no mother sitting next to them.

"I'm still waiting for a new leg," someone else called out.

"We'll get to that. Boys, I know times are tight." Ridley paused. "But this is right."

"What are you running for?" a voice called out.

Heads turned. Ridley looked to the back of the room and saw Harriman staring at him.

"What do you mean, Harry? Don't you think a monument is appropriate?" Ridley spread out his arms to the assembled veterans. "Surely we all agree on that."

"The town square," offered someone.

"How 'bout the Higgins place? Been abandoned for years," chimed in another. Everyone seemed to have an opinion. Ridley raised his hands for quiet.

Harriman called out again. "How about Kennesaw Mountain? Or Shiloh? Or Griswoldville? I can think of a dozen places…"

"Down there?" Ridley spit back, incredulous.

"Where we bled."

Exasperated groans and contemptuous guffaws lacerated his response. Several women glared at Harriman, but kept silent. One woman could not resist asking, "How will we ever see it if it's someplace we'll never get to? None of us ain't ever going down there, that's for sure." Others echoed her sentiment. A few laughs trickled, then died out quickly.

"Who says so?" Harriman retorted.

"Aw, c'mon, Hickenlooper. You know full well no one's goin' down there, unless we have to whip them again," a legless veteran retorted to vigorous laughter.

"That's ridiculous, Harry," Ridley said. "There's no way I'd support erecting a monument in some Rebel backwater."

"We left a lot of men in those backwaters," Harriman answered, fastening a steely glare on Ridley, who avoided it. "It's fitting to remember and acknowledge them where they fell."

"It's Rebel country!" shouted someone from across the room.

"Always will be, too!" Ridley echoed.

"It's still America. President Lincoln would agree with me," Harriman said.

"The traitors got him too, in case you forgot!" Ridley snapped.

The room erupted.

"They're still Americans," Harriman repeated.

The room erupted again.

"They are not!" Ridley bellowed over the uproar. "They forfeited their right, their privilege, to be called Americans when they fired on our flag. If you ask me, we don't owe them anything. They owe us, for committing treason and causing all the death, destruction and suffering they've brought on every family in America. Whatever their plight is now, they deserve every bit of it."

Lucas Rawls stood up and faced Harriman. Lucas had been a family friend for years. A little older than the Hickenlooper brothers, he had sworn to Owen and Molly Hickenlooper that he would look out for their sons when they left for war.

"From what I hear, it's crazy down there. My cousin's in the army in South Carolina and he says the place's all gone to hell. You never backed down from a fight before, Har. You killed Rebs just as dead as any of us. Why're you gettin' soft on them now?"

"I'm not getting soft," Harriman replied. "We fought to preserve the Union. Now that we've won, all I'm hearing is we should treat them like foreigners? If we were divided then, and we're still divided now, what did we accomplish? Was it all for nothing?"

"Give 'em an eye for an eye. Hell, they'd spit on our flag today, just as sure as they did before," hissed Eustis Hoffberger. A black patch covered one eye.

"I bet they want the same things as us. To return to a normal life, to…"

"…move on," Ridley interrupted. "It's time you did too, Harry."

Harriman stared at Ridley.

"Prove it!" hissed Hoffberger.

"How's he gonna do that?" Lucas shrugged.

"I'll bet I can walk the March again," Harriman shot back.

"You're nuts! They'd sooner shoot you as give you the time of day. They ain't never gonna forget our March to the Sea, ain't that right, boys?" Hoffberger clutched excitedly at his pants as if mice were running up them. His one good eye glowered at Harriman as his friends seconded him.

"Do you have the time for this, Harry?" Ridley asked as if he already knew the answer.

"A bet has to have a stake," a voice in the back said.

Heads craned around and found a boy of about seventeen writing and erasing furiously on a piece of paper.

"Who're you?" Lucas asked.

The boy cleared his throat. "My name is Rufus Dewes, sir. I was just clarifying if this is a real bet."

All eyes turned back to Harriman. The room shrank before him. For the longest moment, he stared at the tips of his shoes shuffling on the floor, as if he were practicing dancing with himself. "I'll walk the March again, from Atlanta to Savannah. I'll carry the colors, trusting the people down there to let me pass."

"No way yer touchin' them colors again!" Hoffberger exploded, shaking his fist, his face twisted in fury. "Everyone knows yer off yer rocker, Hickenlooper! I didn't come here to listen to claptrap about marches and monuments. I got me a monument, right here," he snapped, tapping his eye patch. "You ain't carryin' our colors to Georgia as long as I got breath in me! Shame on you! S'cuse me, ladies." Hofberger made for the door. Others followed.

"Hold on there! Don't leave yet," Ridley called out. "Let's give Harry here his due. He was our color bearer after all. The kid's question is a good one. What's the stake, Harry?"

Harriman paused. A grandfather clock in the corner of the room chimed. He seemed to rock backwards at the sounds, as if they'd electrocuted him. He heard himself say, "My farm."

Silence cloaked the room, as if a shotgun had just been fired. The departing veterans stopped in their tracks and turned around. Hofberger shook his head, clucked, spun a finger in the air and plopped down in a chair. This was going to be good.

"Harry, don't you think that's extreme?" Ridley said.

Lucas put a slender, weather-beaten hand on his younger friend's shoulder. "Har, what're you sayin'?"

"I'm saying if I don't come back, Walter here gets my farm. It's practically his now anyway. He bought the note from the bank a few days ago."

"That so, Colonel?" Lucas asked.

There was a surprised murmur in the room. Ridley glared at Harriman and nodded a little nervously.

"If I return," Harriman said, "I get it back, free and clear."

"There will be conditions," Ridley said.

"I expect so."

"Hey, Hickenlooper, why'nt you wear yer old uniform, so's the Rebs don't mistake ya for an idiot!" Hoffberger bellowed. "This is nuts!"

Ridley pondered for a moment and raised a hand. "I'll take your bet. Now, it's best if Harry and I don't take up more time with this matter now. We will work out the details. Let's move on.

Any objections?" There were none. "All right then, let me bring you up to date on the prosthetic arms and legs we have ordered. I have been notified that the prosthesis company is delayed with their next shipment until early next year…" Groans echoed. "I know, I know…"

"Come on, Har," said Lucas. "Let's go."

Veterans stared after Harriman, worry or scorn on their faces, but beneath it, bewilderment. Likely, they wondered what prompted a man who had risked his life so many times in combat to risk all he had left on an absurdly dangerous idea once he was safe at home. Deep down, they knew that the war had changed everybody, somehow.

Rufus Dewes ran up to Harriman and Lucas as they were leaving. "Let me write this story," he said breathlessly. "For the paper."

"What are you talking about? What story?" snapped Harriman. "I'm not doing this to get my name in any newspaper."

"I know, I know, but think of this…" Rufus spread his hands out, reading an imaginary headline. 'VET BETS FARM ON A RETURN TO GLORY.' No, uh, 'VET STAKES FARM ON REBEL GOOD WILL' …something like that. It's a great story, Mr. Hickenlooper. Folks'll wanna know how it turns out. Someone needs to be there to tell them."

"I'm going alone."

"Please, Mr. Hickenlooper, I'd never be in your way. Honest."

"I'm going alone," Harriman repeated and walked out.

Lucas followed after him, but looked back at Rufus, shrugging as if to say, "I know the guy and I don't understand him."

"Why are you doing this?" the boy called out. "Crazy fool." Rufus pulled out his paper and pencil and scribbled furiously, then rushed back into the room. He didn't want to miss any of the hubbub the bet had triggered.

Outside the town hall, the air was clear and cold. It was nearing winter. Harriman mounted his wagon.

"Mind if I come along until we reach the crossroads?" Lucas asked.

Harriman nodded. Lucas tethered his horse to the back of the wagon and climbed in next to Harriman. Overhead, stars shone brightly. The horse's nostrils streamed icy plumes into the November night as it pulled their wagon out of town. Harriman and Lucas rode in silence for a long time, listening to the horse's hooves clopping on the frozen road, staring into the black night under the starry sky.

"Why'dya do go and do that, Har?" Lucas finally asked. "That bet's the dumbest thing I ever heard of."

"I'm going to win it."

"Or die trying. Is that it? Maybe it's easier to give Ridley the chance to do for you what you can't do for yourself."

"What's that, Lucas?"

"Throw in the towel."

"You're my friend, Lucas, but I'm gonna throw you off this wagon if you don't take that back."

"I'm sorry, Har. I didn't mean that."

Harriman snapped the reigns. "Yeah, you did. And maybe you're right. It's not my farm anyway. It's Ridley's. Poppa borrowed to the top in '58. Ridley's been waiting for a reason to snap it up, one that'll look good with the regiment. To foreclose on me might look bad, unless I was crazy and better off without the responsibility."

"Well, aren't ya? Crazy, not better off without it. That farm's all you got left."

"I've got a pile of I.O.U.s is what I've got. No matter, I'm going to win the bet..."

They spoke in unison. "...Or die trying."

Lucas saw the T in the road coming up none too soon. He jumped off the wagon and mounted his horse. "Guess I can't talk you out of it."

"You guessed right."

"Let me come with ya, then?"

"This trip's getting real popular. No sense in two fools dying. It'd be better if you looked after things 'til I got back." Harriman chuckled. "Do a damn sight better job of it. What's today? The seventeenth, right? Didn't we set off from Atlanta about then?"

"I guess."

"It took us five weeks doing fifteen miles a day, carrying a full pack through Rebel country. This time, it's just me and that flag."

"It's still Rebbie country!" Lucas exhaled deeply, gathering in his temper. "Y'aint gonna take the flag, are ya? Boys'd be mighty peeved. Truth is, I would be, too."

"I carried it when they were shooting at us!"

"They'll still be shootin' at ya! Har, listen. We both know how bad we wrecked Georgia. Rebs surely ain't forgotten. How could they? If it were my home and they'd done what we done, I wouldn't be forgettin' any time soon. Carryin' a shot-up battle flag in yer old uniform, yer a walkin' bulls-eye, an' salt in the wound. Har, listen to me. There ain't gonna be nobody to help ya..." His words drifted off in the stiffening wind.

"I have to do this, understand?"

"No, I don't understand. An' even if I did, I'd still be dead set against it."

In that moment, Lucas felt the dread he'd heard men speak of time and time again during the war. It would come before a charge against massed artillery over an open field, but it would just as easily come before setting out on patrol, or even just waking up on a clear, sunny morning to cook breakfast during a break in a campaign. It didn't matter when it came. What did matter was what it said: "Your number's up." Every soldier believed it down to his soul when he heard it. It was never wrong. Lucas had never felt it himself. Until now. "Think about it a little more, will ya?"

Harriman stared at him and said nothing.

"Well, at least let me know when you're goin'. I'll take ya to the train. Okay?" Lucas mounted his horse and snapped the reins. As he trotted away, he turned around and saw Harriman standing there, watching him go into the dark, clear night. Lucas turned back quickly, hunkered down in the saddle and pulled up his coat.

Harriman went into the farmhouse and let his coat slip to the floor amidst the clothes, tools and papers. Going into his bedroom, he pulled out a large, weather-beaten trunk wrapped in large leather straps from under his bed. The trunk was stuck fast, so he worked it for a few moments until he got it open. He pulled out a dusty blue uniform, a leather-bound book and a bundle wrapped in oilcloth. He swept aside more clothes from the bed and laid these things out, then hauled out a dirty, faded army shoulder pack. Searching around the room, he noticed a small, faded American flag on a sewing block...

"Momma, we have to go. We can't be late for muster. Momma, where are you?"

Molly Hickenlooper entered, carrying a bag.

Lucas Rawls put his hand on Harriman's shoulder. "We have a little time, Mrs. Hickenlooper."

"Thank you, Lucas. Boys, I've put together a few things for your journey." Molly Hickenlooper pushed the glasses that perched perpetually and precariously on the edge of her nose and placed a large bag in front of the two brothers and Lucas.

"Momma, I can't take that. The Colonel said we only get to take a few personal things, we've got to travel light."

"I don't care what Mr. Granger said. These will come in handy." She smiled at her sons wistfully and sighed as she withdrew socks, a shirt, toiletries. She gamely pushed the tears back as she packed some other things into the bag.

"Oh, Momma, please don't worry. This'll all be over in ninety days."

"It isn't that." Molly moved to the sewing table by the hearth and caressed a small American flag sitting on her sewing block. "The thing I wanted you to take with you more than anything else, and I haven't finished it."

Owen Hickenlooper came in and took Lucas aside.

"I have known you a long time, Lucas Rawls, and I have never asked you for anything. Ever."

"Yes, sir."

"I'm asking you now. You watch out for my boys, you hear?"

"Yes, sir. I will."

Harriman and Alonzo surrounded their mother with their arms.
"Please don't fret. I'll take the flag the way it is," Harriman said.

"No, you will not. You will have a proper flag. I will finish it
and send it to you."

"Momma, you don't have to…"

"Yes, I do."

Harriman ran his hands over the cloth, tracing his mother's
fine embroidery and the empty cloth where she hadn't finished.
He dug further into his trunk and found his rubber poncho and
army blanket. He shoved them and some clothes inside the pack.
A wave of fatigue engulfed him. He swept the pack onto the floor,
lay down on the bed he'd been born in and tumbled into a deep,
troubled sleep.

CHAPTER 7

As he rode down Main Street, Harriman noticed folks weren't doing the usual—seeing him and looking away in pity. Usually people would see him coming and maybe nod as he passed by, but were unwilling to make conversation. Today he thought they were looking at him more closely, almost as if they were seeing him for the first time. He saw them whisper, figuring they'd heard about the bet. That was surely something to talk about. That he was more than ever their focus made him want to crack the reins and get the horses galloping out of town, out of sight.

He stared past them and reached the entrance of the Farmers and Mechanics Bank. He kept an eye out for dogs, then jumped off and walked into the bank. It was empty except for Walter Ridley. From his desk behind a large glass divider, Ridley made no move to greet him.

"Had a chance to reconsider?" Ridley asked.

"I want it all in writing, everything we agree on."

"You have my word on it. That's good enough between soldiers."

"It isn't good enough between you and me."

Ridley pretended to ignore the slight and took out a pen and paper. "It isn't that easy to write such a thing, especially on short notice."

"You have a way with words. They're your conditions, not mine."

Ridley nodded. "True." He twirled the pen in his hand. He got up to wind a clock perched on the mantel behind him. "I'll write what we agree to and we will sign it. I will keep it in the safe until you return."

"I'll read it first, then if it's acceptable, I'll sign it. We each get one copy. Lucas Rawls gets one, too."

"Corporal Rawls? What's he got to do with this?" Ridley snapped.

"He's my friend. And he's my witness."

"All of Centerville is your witness. You don't need another."

"What are the conditions?"

The door swung open and Lucas entered. "G'mornin'. Har, Colonel. Sorry I'm late. Had some things to do."

"Come in, Corporal." Ridley sighed and began to write, speaking out loud as he did. "I will need tangible proof that you made the march. This is a real wager, and a serious stake." He looked up at Harriman, who simply nodded. "I was impressed by your faith in Southern good will. You should go unarmed, don't you think?"

Again, Harriman nodded.

"Wha..?" Lucas spluttered. "C'mon!"

Harriman raised a hand to calm his friend and said. "What else?"

Ridley kept writing, a grin barely discernible. "I would assume that, being treated as an American, you would come back unharmed, untouched by ill-will?"

"Yes."

"How much time do you need?"

"We did it in thirty-seven days the last time."

"Yes, I recall." Ridley swiveled in his chair and examined a calendar hanging on the wall behind him. "I'll give you an extra week. Let's say New Year's Day. A fine way to usher in a New Year. Sound fair?"

"Agreed."

A customer entered. "I'll be right with you, Mrs. Schultz. One last thing." Ridley paused. "I will need evidence, something tangible, that proves you made this march according to the terms we've agreed to here."

"I'll find something." Harriman's steady gaze unnerved Ridley.

Ridley wrote it down. "You know, Harry, some people think you've gone crazy."

"Maybe. Maybe I'm just putting myself out of my misery. Some people might call that sane." Harriman leaned toward Ridley. "Or maybe I'm just squaring our accounts."

"What do you mean by that?"

"You know damned well what I mean."

For a moment, the two locked eyes. Ridley looked away and pushed the paper across the desk. "All right, then."

When Harriman read it and nodded his assent, Ridley wrote out two more copies, then pushed them over for Harriman to sign.

Harriman signed and handed the pen to Lucas. "You sign it, too. As my witness."

Ridley rose abruptly from his chair and moved past Harriman. "Good morning. What can I do for you today, Mrs. Schultz?"

"I guess we're done here," Lucas said.

CHAPTER 8

"**H**ow much?"

Jakob Dreisler ran his wrinkled old hands over the smooth back of the cow, jingling the bell around her neck. "I give you twenty dollars, though she pushes on the years."

Harriman nodded. "Could you see yourself to twenty-five?"

"I do you kindness to buy her at all. She might be dry this time next year." Jakob looked around the Hickenlooper farm for a moment. "See, forget this silly bet. Stay home. Your folks would be wanting you to make good on this place."

Harriman offered his hand. "Twenty it is for the cow. The nag here is still solid. I'll take thirty for her."

"You selling everything, boy?"

"Enough for the trains, provisions and lodgings. Enough to get there and back. I know you'll take good care of them. Perhaps I could buy them back when I return." He smiled at Jakob.

"Fine, fine." Dreisler shook his head as he counted out the money and handed it to Harriman. "This is bad business, this bet."

He pulled on the cow's lead and hitched it and the horses' reins to his wagon, then mounted it.

Harriman looked at the greenbacks in his hand. "Mr. Dreisler, this is more than I asked for."

"Come back safe, boy." Jakob Dreisler waved over his shoulder, the cowbell clanking in time to her steps.

"Bye, old girl." Harriman watched her go. "I sure won't miss that bell."

CHAPTER 9

Rufus paced in front of the office door, stepping around piles of newspapers on the floor. Dust particles swirled in the sunlight that poured through the windows of Centerville's paper, *The Loyal Citizen*. Since the reunion, all he could think about was the story:

A veteran, walking unarmed across the South, bets all he has left in life on the good will of the Southern people to help him find a monument for Union dead and to reach Savannah unharmed, all to reaffirm his belief in one people, one country.

Terrific! It was a story every Iowan would read. He knew it was.

Behind that door was the man who could make it possible for people to read his story. It burst open. Jack Connolly loomed over Rufus, his beefy frame filling the doorway, waving a clutch of papers. "Miss Rutledge, where are my spectacles?" A prim woman, Irma Rutledge, looked up from her work in the corner.

"They're on your forehead," Rufus said, pointing.

"I didn't ask you," Connolly said, feeling for his glasses. "Who're you?"

"I want to cover the story about the Sixth Iowa."

"What're you talking about? What story?"

"The one about Harriman Hickenlooper's bet, you know, marching across Georgia and finding a monument and..."

The editor of the *The Loyal Citizen* held up a big hand and cut him short.

Rufus silently cursed his garbled words. He imagined Connolly reading what he had just blubbered and throwing it, and him, in the trash.

"Slow down! What happened?" Connolly demanded.

Rufus' memorized pitch speech mercifully came back to him and in painstaking detail, he described the bet and the raucous uproar it provoked.

"I bet it did. Sounds like this Hickenlooper's down on his luck and out of his mind."

"And his farm. No one thinks he'll make it back. There's more. Mr. Ridley bought the note on it from his own bank."

"What? How'd you know that?"

"Hickenlooper said so. Ridley didn't deny it, either. Word around town is, Hickenlooper has been late on payments." Dewes started to pace again. "It didn't seem Ridley was too keen on talking about it in front of the regiment. Nobody's business, I guess."

"Least of all yours." Connolly paused for a moment, then grabbed Dewes by the arm. "Come in and sit down. What's your name again?"

"I didn't tell you yet. It's Rufus Dewes, sir."

"What kind of name is Rufus? Where're you from, Rufus? You're not local, are you?" Connolly didn't wait for an answer, but walked back into the glass-partitioned office, sat down and propped his feet up on the desk. His glasses slid lower on his forehead. "There bad blood between these two?"

"I don't know, sir. That's one of the things I'll find out."

"How will you do that?"

"Go with him."

"He's deranged and so are you."

"Wait a minute, sir. I have talked to several men in the regiment. They don't claim to know anything about any bad blood between them.

Or else they're not willing to talk about it. And you'd think they would. They've been through everything together. My sense is, they just can't figure it."

"Your sense, eh? How old are you, lad?"

"Nineteen."

Connolly grunted, tapping his fingers on the desk. "What's the bet again? Tell it to me again."

When Dewes had finished, Connolly rose from his chair. "Someone needs to talk him out of this!"

"Why? I told him it was a great story and I should go with him to write it."

"You tried to convince him to let you go with him? Well, well." The youth smiled broadly.

"Dewes, did you stop to think that the war is over now? There's no use digging up old wounds. No one cares a lick about what's going on in Georgia, or anywhere else south of the Mason Dixon. What matters is life in Centerville, Iowa. How about convincing him not to go at all? Hell, I'll talk to him."

"You can't." Rufus regretted it the moment he said it.

"The hell I can't! I don't like being told what I can and can't do, especially by some kid lying about his age to get a job...Why not?"

"Because he had that look in his eye. The one that says 'I'll walk over you if you try to stop me.' Excuse me, sir, but I didn't see you at the reunion."

"Because I wasn't there. I was attending to my wife. She is not well."

"I'm sorry to hear that."

Connolly hesitated. "Those conditions of the bet, that he go unarmed, untouched by misfortune, whatever. How do you know that?"

"I spoke to Lucas Rawls. He was Hickenlooper's witness to the written terms of the wager. He couldn't believe the terms either."

"They're full of Walter's sense of humor."

"Someone else at the reunion even suggested he wear his old uniform."

"Another brilliant idea. Why would he do that?"

"So, and I quote, the Rebs wouldn't mistake him for an idiot. I think he meant it as a joke. But he wants to take the regiment's battle flag with him."

Connolly shook his head. "This man is truly mad!" He took in a breath and folded his hands. "What did Ridley mean by 'untouched'?"

"Unharmed, I guess." Rufus glanced at Miss Rutledge, who was watching their exchange intently. "So you're interested in this story, Mr. Connolly?"

"Lad, I've got work to do, so one word of advice. Go home, go to school, get a job, but whatever you do, forget about this madness."

"But you are interested, right?"

"If you'll excuse me..."

Dewes waited for a sign the grizzled editor might relent. When none came, he scribbled some notes on his ever-present notepad, turned and left the office without another word.

"Miss Rutledge, find me the profiles I wrote on Walter Ridley and Damon Granger for the regimental election. It would have been around the time the Sixth was formed, summer of '61."

"Yes, Mr. Connolly. July of 1861." Miss Rutledge waited.

"Yes, what is it?" Connolly asked.

"Did you want anything else?"

"Like what?"

"Perhaps something on Sherman's March to the Sea. Or Harriman Hickenlooper's family. It seems like there are a lot of places to start."

"Very well."

Connolly sat down at his desk, letting out an audible sigh. The world was still going mad, even after five years of total war. He was afraid he was going mad as well, day after agonizing day witnessing his dear Ruthie wither away from something the doctors could not describe, except by their expressions when they tried to. It was a matter of time. So who was to say what was worse, waiting for death to come, lying in a bed, or inviting it to follow a crazy principle down Georgia's back roads?

He had to admit, something in the story did pique his interest. His dear Ruthie's drawn, withered face called him home. "Miss Rutledge, I'm going home. Where're my glasses?"

"They were on your forehead the last time I saw them," came the reply.

He rolled his chair away from his desk to the crunching of glass underneath him.

CHAPTER 10

Harriman awoke before dawn. The sun cast a first warm hint over the frigid horizon, throwing jagged golden slivers across the ceiling through the uneven cracks in the log walls. Being so alert surprised him, because for the first time in a long while, he awoke free of any fallout from the nightmares that lurked under the surface of first sleep. Usually they grew in ever-increasing dread until either he had to wake up or die the same miserable death. He would then lie staring at the ceiling until first light. This pattern would inevitably cause him to fall asleep at odd times of the day, interrupting his chores. Growing up, first light used to be the best time, when his world was purest. The days would move from one clear, waking moment to the next, measured by the things he needed to do for the farm, and always free of charge.

A picture of his parents sat on the fireplace mantle. His parents were not in the typical pose of the times—husband standing, wife sitting—but standing side by side. He stared at them, but then panicked for an instant when all he saw were two faded faces frozen into the daguerreotype. Worst of all, he couldn't remember the sound of their voices.

He got dressed, went outside to the family plot and knelt by his parents' graves in order to feel them closer. He prayed for something to bring their faces, their smells, their voices, some sense of them, back to him. What he heard was the faint creaking of wheels on Lucas Rawls' wagon approaching. He returned to the house to finish packing.

Lucas entered the farmhouse and spotted the Navy Colt .56 revolver on the bed.

"Yer takin' that, right?"

"No. I'm finished with guns. Besides, the bet says I go unarmed. It was in my things, but if you want it, you keep it. In fact, take whatever you need."

"At least take it to protect yerself, Har. Ridley'll never know."

"I will be protected myself, but not by that. You know where the feed is. I ran out of nails for the fence sections. Maybe if you need more, you could pick them up and put it on my bill. No, forget that, Mr. Cummins won't stand for it. Here's some feed money for the animals. I sold one of the horses and the cow, so don't be worrying she's wandered off or dead somewhere."

"What's this?" Lucas asked, holding up an oilcloth-wrapped packet lying next to Harriman's bag.

"Nothing."

"Why're you packing it?"

"Just something I've got to return."

"Return? To who? You'd be the first person I know made a friend on the March."

Harriman took the oilcloth from Lucas without explaining further, looked around his room one last time, then closed his Union Army pack and walked out.

They set off in silence. As they passed the Centerville Town Hall, Harriman made Lucas pull up on the reins.

"Why're we stopping here?" Lucas asked.

Harriman hopped off and entered the hall. Lucas followed. Inside, tied to a staff in a corner of the room stood the torn and tattered battle flag of the Sixth Iowa. Centerville women had sewed into the fabric names of the engagements the regiment had fought—Shiloh, Vicksburg, Big Black River, Kennesaw Mountain, Atlanta, and more. Harriman stared at it a long moment, lost somewhere in the names. He reached for the flag.

Lucas grabbed Harriman's arm and inserted himself between Harriman and the flag. "No!"

"It was okay to carry it when people were shooting at me, but this is different?"

"Yer damn straight this is different! That flag's a whole lot bigger than this damn fool bet." For a moment, they lingered as close to blows as they had ever come. "C'mon. Leave it, Har," Lucas implored.

Harriman turned and walked back to the wagon. He took out his mother's unfinished flag from his pocket and tied it to his walking stick. "This'll do."

"The hell's that?" Lucas examined the small flag.

"Momma was sewing it for me."

"Ah." Lucas snapped the reins.

The wagon rolled down Main Street, the early morning mist shrouding the windows and roofs. As they passed the bakery, Harriman jumped off the wagon again and headed around the back of the building.

"What're you doin' now?" Lucas called out after him, pulling the horses to a stop. "Nothin's open."

"Wait here."

Harriman climbed the outside stairs, entered and walked to the door at the end of the hall. He knocked and waited, then knocked again.

"Who's there?" The door cracked open and Dewes poked his head out. "Mr. Hickenlooper? What're you doing here?"

"If you're coming, snap to it."

Dewes' eyes lit up, a giant grin spreading across his face. "Come in, come in, please."

His small room was a mess of newspapers, books, articles and maps, the jetsam of Dewes' obsession with a war he had missed out on, crammed and growing like weeds over every available surface.

The youth stuffed his things into a small canvas bag, ran out of space and started over. Harriman made a big show of rising to leave. "I'm almost finished!" Rufus yelped.

Watching the youth figure out what he needed amused Harriman. He, like all veterans, had learned quickly—on twenty-mile forced marches over all kinds of terrain, under the worst weather—what one could and should carry, and still keep up the pace with enough energy to go right into a fight if necessary. On the March to the Sea, they'd covered three hundred miles in five weeks with small packs. Rufus was packing for a trek in the African bush for a year.

"That's enough," Harriman said finally. "Now, listen. There's one other thing."

"Yes, sir."

"If you come, you agree that whatever I tell you to do, you do. No questions."

"As long as I can write down anything I see and hear, and whatever you tell me I can send it back to Mr. Connolly at *The Loyal Citizen*." He carefully folded a large map into a shoulder bag and threw it over his back.

"What's that?"

"It's a map done by Orlando Poe, Sherman's Chief of Engineers. He made a complete map and chronicle of the March. It can't hurt to know where you're going, right?" Rufus examined his room one last time so he could regret now what he would sorely miss later.

"Say it," Harriman said.

Rufus met his stare. "Say what?"

"Your answer to my condition."

"Oh, yes, I agree. Now you say it. You agree I can write down whatever you tell me and send it to Mr. Connolly?"

"Agreed," Harriman said.

"Who's he? What's he doin'?" Lucas exclaimed, watching Rufus climb on the back of the wagon. "Criminy, Har. He can't go with you! He's a kid, for Pete's sake!"

"He's nineteen. I was younger than that when I killed my first Rebel."

"Sheeit, nineteen! You b'lieve that?"

"I am nineteen!" Rufus exclaimed.

"See," Harriman said.

"However the hell old you say you are, no one's old enough to go on this foolish thing."

Harriman grinned. "The boy's made up his mind."

"That's right, sir," Rufus answered. "I'm going to write about the Second March to the Sea."

"Harriman Hickenlooper, if somethin' happens to him, it's on your head. It's one thing to do a stupid thing on your account, but to drag this boy into it." He turned to Rufus. "What's yer momma say 'bout this?"

"I don't have a mother."

"Kid's going to help me win this bet. Come on. We have a train to catch."

They rode on out of town, the creaking wagon wheels the only sound for a long time. It was midway to the station before Lucas finally asked, "You remember the first time you saw the elephant?"

"I've never been to a circus," Rufus chimed in. "I'd sure like to, though. I had a dog once."

"'Seeing the elephant' is what comes over you the first time someone shoots at you," Harriman explained.

"Oh."

"Or get that feeling about your number bein' up?" Lucas stared ahead.

"Nope. I never did get that one, or I probably wouldn't be here. Hey, that's no way to send us off." Harriman elbowed his friend.

They rode the rest of the way in silence. When they reached the Burlington depot, Harriman and Rufus hopped off. Lucas started to get down, too.

"You best get on back," Harriman said quickly. "Thanks for bringing us to the train."

"Hunh." Lucas's voice was choked. "Well, take care a yerselves, I guess."

They shook hands heartily. But as they walked onto the station platform, Lucas caught up with his friend and wrapped him in a long embrace. A train whistle sounded off in the distance.

For one last moment, Harriman gazed at his friend, fixing him in his memory forever.

"Don' worry, I'll take care of the farm," Lucas gulped.

"Thanks, friend. I know you will."

He watched Lucas climb onto the wagon and whip the reins smartly. The horses responded, clacking down the cobblestone streets of Burlington.

Turning back, he met the eager young face of Rufus Dewes. He smiled. The train whistle blew and steam hissed, announcing its arrival.

"First ride on a train?"

"Actually, it is, sir."

"Come on then."

They grabbed their bags and got on board.

CHAPTER II

The further south it traveled, the more the train filled with
the debris of Reconstruction: carpetbaggers seeking new
opportunities; occupation soldiers—mostly boys sour they were
policing a land destroyed before they got a chance to get into the
Big Fight; families going from nowhere to anywhere else.

For long stretches, Harriman kept his eyes glued on the
landscape, listening to the steady, slow clacking of the wheels on rails.

Dewes spent a lot of time alternately writing in his journal and
drifting in and out of sleep.

Somewhere over the Tennessee line, Harriman nudged him with
his foot.

"Hunh?"

"How old are you?"

"How old are you?" Rufus replied.

"Listen, the only reason you're here is because I invited you. You
don't get to be smart with me."

"I told you already. I'm nineteen."

"And I'm Robert E. Lee." Harriman pointed a finger at him.
"Don't lie to me."

"Jeez. I'm seventeen."

"If you were so keen on this war, why didn't you join up?"

"I tried, believe me," Rufus answered bitterly. "My stupid mother wouldn't let me. My Poppa died at Stones River, so I guess I was all she had left. Twice I tried, but the recruiters needed her permission and she'd never give it. I should have just run away."

"I thought you said you didn't have a mother."

"I don't. I mean, I don't ever see her."

"So now you want to write about a war you didn't get to fight?"

"It's more than that. I've wanted to be a reporter since I was a boy."

"You're still a boy."

"I like hearing and telling stories. I collect and read whatever I can about the war—newspapers, memoirs, speeches. My favorite thing is listening to the veterans recount their stories on the porch of Mr. Tompkins' store."

"That's where I've seen you before."

"I've seen you around, too. You don't get along with that dog."

Harriman grunted.

"I imagine I'm interviewing the veterans for some paper where my name is in the byline, front page. Whenever one of the veterans starts going on, it's like I'm right there in it with him. It's me living his story. I imagine what I would have done in that critical moment. By the way, why'd you change your mind? Why did you let me come with you?"

"Figured you could attest to what happened, help me get the farm back."

"Anyway, my mother took to drink and started doing things I didn't like, so I left home. I work odd jobs, but just about every town has a newspaper, so I always ask the editors to give me a chance. No luck so far." Rufus stared off at the passing scenery, intermittently writing in his diary.

"Why'd you want to fight?"

"To put down the Great Rebellion, of course."

"So coming with me, you'll see what you missed."

"Well, sort of. At least I'll see some of what you saw."

A conductor entered the car and announced the next stop: Chattanooga, Tennessee.

"You were here, right?" Rufus asked. Harriman nodded. Rufus continued. "It was here to Chattanooga that Rosecrans had retreated after getting whipped by Longstreet at Chickamauga. And where he got trapped with an army he couldn't feed. There was no way to re-start an invasion of Georgia until his army could be relieved and re-supplied."

Harriman was impressed at the boy's knowledge, and was glad he'd followed his instinct to bring him along. "Go on." His eyes fixed on the city coming into view in the valley below and its surrounding hills.

"Well, public opinion had already forgotten our victories at Gettysburg and Vicksburg in July 1863 because soon after an invasion of the South through Tennessee failed. Worse, the Union Army of the Cumberland got itself trapped inside Chattanooga and was starving. Lincoln sent Ulysses Grant, who'd engineered the six-month siege and capture of Vicksburg, to relieve it and commence another invasion into Georgia. Grant quickly sized up the situation. Typically, where others had dithered, or worried about what the Rebels were doing, Grant ordered an attack."

CHAPTER 12

"We couldn't believe the General's order," Harriman recalled.

"Why not? Grant always took the offensive."

"No. Somehow the orders we got called for us to seize the rifle pits at the base of the ridge, nothing more."

"Missionary Ridge," Rufus interjected.

"That damned ridge, the one that looks out on the city, hell, the entire valley. From there the Rebs blasted any supply column that tried to make it into Chattanooga. We were eating the dogs. Another reason I don't like them. After you've tasted them…

"After we got the order to attack, I wrote my name and address on a paper and had my brother pin it on my back. I did the same for him. That way the burial details would know how to notify my folks. We took the rifle pits at the base of the ridge. Once we got there, we grabbed any food the Rebels had left behind. You'd have thought we had just routed the whole Rebel army. Ridley ordered us to hold and wait for further orders.

"It wasn't long before Reb artillery found the range and began to hit the rifle pits we were sitting in. We were unable to attack and afraid to run away. Some men panicked and broke for the rear just the same. My brother Alonzo was watching the Rebels we'd rousted from the rifle pits scattering up the steep ridge with those Rebel shells getting closer. 'What're we stoppin' for? We got 'em on the run! C'mon, Har, let's get 'em!' he yelled and just grabbed me. Before I knew it, we were chasing after the Rebs scrambling up the ridge toward their trenches. A few other men followed us, figuring it was better than being blown to bits sitting on our butts. Shells were landing all around us. One shell took our color bearer's head clean off...

"I, uh, I picked up the flag and chased my brother up that hill. I heard later Ridley was angry his men disobeyed his orders. He'd even drawn his sword and pistol and threatened boys if they joined the attack. They did anyway.

"I heard also that Colonel Granger publicly reminded Ridley that officers led from the front, and proceeded to follow his men up the ridge. I can just see Ridley standing in that trench alone, shells landing closer to him all the time, his orders drowned out by the cheers of the boys running past him up the slope. Something must have convinced Ridley to move up the ridge rather than follow orders.

"I remember Alonzo catching up to a pudgy Rebel officer scrambling up the ridge, gasping for air, and yelling something like, 'C'mon, Johnny! First one to the top wins the war!' Alonzo swatted the officer's hat off his head and put it on. The Reb pulled his pistol. When I saw him do that, I threw the flagstaff full into the man's back and dropped him before he could put one in my brother. Alonzo, he just kept on going. 'Owe you one, Har!' he yelled as he disappeared up the hill into the smoke. Only time I ever dropped the flag...I still have that Reb's pistol."

"You brought it with you, right?" Rufus asked.

"Nope. Unarmed, remember? It's part of the bet. Thing was, the Rebs at the top of the ridge couldn't see through that smoke either, but they could sure hear the shrieks of their comrades and us driving them like cattle. So when the Rebs approached the top, their comrades on the crest were waving 'em in. Then they saw us coming out of the smoke right behind. And when they did, they couldn't fire at us without first shooting down their own men. Our Spencers and Henrys could shoot down both and because they're repeaters, at a much faster clip. Before their officers could rally them, the Rebels were scattering down the back slope. We surged over the top and ran out of steam.

"When Ridley got to the top, the first thing he saw was Alonzo guarding the hatless Rebel colonel and thirty other Rebs, wearing the biggest grin I ever saw. Alonzo said, 'It's your honor, Har.'

"I saluted Colonel Ridley. When he returned my salute, I saw a hateful look in his eyes. I never forgot that look. But I didn't care. I walked to a rocky outcropping and planted the Stars and Stripes. From up there, I could see other Union battle flags fluttering all along the ridgeline. I still hear the cheers that went up from our boys in the valley below.

"Ridley ordered us to organize the prisoners. He never once looked at Alonzo or me. He talked to that Reb officer who'd lost his hat enough."

"Did you hear what he said?"

"No, but I imagine him saying how rough it had been, in front of the charge."

"Was Ridley a coward?"

"What do you think?"

"Sounds like it."

"He'd say he was just following orders."

CHAPTER 13

"Excuse me. Is this seat taken?" asked a stocky, well-dressed man sporting an earnest grin.

Harriman pushed his hat over his eyes, scanned the many other empty seats in the car, then shrugged. The man took the seat across from him.

"Where're ya headed?" the man asked.

"Savannah," Harriman replied. "You?"

"Atlanta. Great town, Savannah. Intact, pretty much. Sherman musta had a girlie there." The man chuckled. "What takes you there?"

Harriman hesitated. He knew he'd be asked this question again and again, but wasn't expecting it so soon. "I have business."

"What kind of business do you do?"

"I'm a farmer."

"How about you, son?" the man asked Rufus.

"I'm a writer," Rufus replied, holding up his diary.

Harriman smiled, registering the man's confusion.

The man plowed on, noting Hickenlooper's blue overcoat and the flag wrapped on his stick next to him. "Where're you from, if you don't mind me asking?"

"Iowa."

"Never been to Iowa. Farthest north I ever got was Kentucky. I'm going to Atlanta. I'm a salesman. Name's Miles Brockenbrough." He thrust out a hand, which Harriman shook, and then he handed Harriman a card. Harriman glanced at it politely and put it in his pocket.

The man leaned over to see what Rufus was writing. Dewes covered his diary and turned his shoulder to the man. Harriman watched passing fields and forests through the window. Occasionally, he caught a glimpse of some farmer hitched to a plow trailing a sorry-looking horse, or ragged, dirty children waving from the side of the tracks.

"Ever been to Atlanta?" Brockenbrough asked.

"Once, during the war."

Brockenbrough registered that. "Place is coming back good now. What brings you down here?"

"I made a bet I could make the march from Atlanta to Savannah again."

"Hunh. One of Sherman's boys. Getting sentimental, are you?"

Rufus glared at Brockenbrough, who kept smiling at Harriman as if he'd flattered him.

"Something like that," Harriman answered evenly.

The train pulled into a rebuilt Atlanta station. Brockenbrough rose and gathered his things. "I have lots of friends between Atlanta and Savannah. It's my territory."

"Been working it long?" Harriman asked.

"Long enough. Feel free to use my name if you ever need anything. Chances are, someone'll know me." He gave another card to Rufus as he left the railcar.

Rufus crumpled it up and tossed it on the floor. "I don't like that man."

"Could have fooled me." Harriman cracked a smile.

Harriman had no sooner set foot in Atlanta than he wanted out. Its noise and bustle made him anxious. It seemed that everything was either being built or being demolished to be built again. He had no curiosity about how the city had been rebuilt, just how it had been wrecked.

He and Rufus stopped in a general store. The women moved away from him as soon as they saw him enter. They gathered some provisions and waited. It seemed to take a long time, and when the shopkeeper had finished with his previous customer, he moved away from Harriman as if he weren't there. Harriman placed his goods on the counter in front of the man. "What's the best way to get to the Macon road?"

The shopkeeper sized him up while glancing at the other customers who were moving away from the man in blue. Then he motioned Hickenlooper aside and quietly gave him directions. Hickenlooper paid his bill and left. Out on the street, it wasn't minutes before another man stopped them.

"You look like men of eminent good sense. I happen to have in my pocket a unique and surefire way to make your fortune."

"And what's that?" Rufus asked.

"Crisp, clean newly printed shares of the Atlanta and Western Railroad."

"It's been rebuilt?" Harriman asked.

"As we speak. That's what the money's for. It was destroyed in the recent unpleasantness, but will be operational before you know it. With your help, we'll make it better than before. Atlanta's on the move. Mighty proud of that. Perhaps I could offer you a drink and we could discuss our business privately."

"Sorry, things are tight right now."

Harriman and Rufus walked to a nearby hotel and went into a small bar off the main lobby. A contingent of Union Army officers and enlisted men were milling around, laughing. Harriman went to the bar with his back to the Yankees and ordered a drink for himself.

"Gee, thanks, Mr. Hickenlooper. I can drink too, you know," Rufus said sourly.

"Sure." Harriman glanced at the group of soldiers in the mirror facing the bar. He wasn't liking what he heard.

A major sat with his spit-shined boots propped up on the table, regaling the junior officers and enlisted men. "…It was so hot, you could fry an egg on the street. Flames rose three hundred feet high in the sky. Folks said Atlanta burned for five days. Hood blamed the fire on Sherman. Hood'd lost an arm at Gettysburg and a leg somewhere else, I forget. Uncle Billy called him a limbless liar." The junior officers forced a laugh. The major caught Harriman watching him in the mirror. "You. What're you doing there? You're supposed to salute an officer."

"I mustered out," Harriman replied.

"When? What regiment?"

Harriman replied slowly, "July 25, 1865. Sixth Iowa Volunteer Infantry, 2nd Brigade, 1st Division, Army of the Tennessee. You were in the Atlanta campaign? What was your regiment, sir?"

The major bristled. "What's it to you?" The officer noted Harriman's faded uniform and the flag by his side. "What're you doing here? War's over, or didn't you know?" More forced laughter.

"I'm walking to Savannah."

"That's a long walk. What on earth for?"

"I bet someone in my old outfit I could make the march again."

A squat old sergeant whistled. "You came all the way here for that? You best turn around and mind your turnips, boyo. This surely ain't no place for reminiscin'."

"Thanks for the advice." Harriman downed the rest of his drink, tossed money on the bar and walked over to the officer. The sergeant stepped between them.

"At ease, Sergeant," the major said.

Harriman leaned down and whispered into the major's ear. "Since you didn't tell me your unit, I'll take it to mean you were never in the Atlanta campaign. I'd be more careful about the stories you tell. Someone might remember things differently." Harriman nodded at the officer and walked out.

The major blanched, stared straight ahead and swallowed his drink.

"What's that about, sir? Should I arrest him?" the sergeant asked.

"Nothing, Sergeant," said the major, removing his boots from the table. "Get the men organized. We move out in ten minutes."

The color bearer and reporter were soon on the Macon road. They walked it for a long time. No one noticed them, or if they did, made nothing of it. It wasn't like the last time Harriman had walked the road. He remembered the banter of his comrades as they left Atlanta and the smell of thick black smoke still rising from it as they marched south and east.

There wasn't a man in Sherman's army who knew what their destination was except for the general himself and certain of his staff. Was it due east, to Augusta, where some of the South's largest remaining gunpowder factories were? Or southeast, to seize the state capitol at Milledgeville? Or, as many hoped, southwest, to liberate the prison camp at Andersonville? There, forty thousand of their Union brethren were prisoners of war, starving and dying daily by the dozens in a camp built for a quarter of that number. The one direction nobody wanted to go was north, back the way they had come.

What set every Union man's heart pounding with a mixture of apprehension and excitement as they marched out of Atlanta in three columns sixty miles wide that November day was the battle order Sherman had issued them. "…Make fifteen miles a day and forage liberally off the land."

Georgia was going to howl. The Army of the Tennessee would make sure of it.

CHAPTER 14

Harriman sat under a tree, closed his eyes and felt the sun against his face in the crisp November air. Rufus started whistling "Marching Through Georgia."

"Stop," Harriman said.

"Why?"

"Because you can bet no one around here would appreciate it."

"Got that right," a voice seconded him.

They turned and saw a tall, wiry man standing by the side of the road, squinting at them with steady eyes shaded by a torn brown slouch hat.

"What're you doin' here?" the man asked.

"I'm—we're—going to Savannah," said Harriman.

"Walkin'?"

Harriman nodded.

"S' fair walk."

"I've done it before."

The man nodded and fixed his gaze on Harriman's dusty, tattered uniform. He also noticed the walking stick with a small flag attached to it propped up against the tree. "Mind if I ask why?"

Harriman explained the wager. The man listened, letting his eyes drift back to the flagstaff. Rufus wrote in his diary.

"What was yer outfit?"

"Sixth Iowa Infantry, Army of the Tennessee. Harriman Hickenlooper." He extended a hand. None came back.

"Iowa, hunh? John Jordan. You been travelin' long?"

Harriman gazed at the afternoon sky. "All day, pretty much. I lost track of time, truthfully."

"My place's jes down the road. Care to whet yer whistle?"

"Thanks."

They walked down the dusty lane for some time, finding nothing to say.

Finally, Jordan asked a few clarifying questions about the wager, and cackled at the answers. "Long odds, I'm afraid. We're here."

They arrived at a shack with a rusting tin roof nestled amid tall trees and set off some ways from the road. A young woman, old for her time, was hanging clothes on a wash line in the front yard. Two young children darted cheerfully between her skirts and the drying clothes. The woman looked up and saw the stranger's blue uniform and flag. She made no move to greet him. The children ran to their father and hugged him. He laughed and hugged them back.

"Sally, this here's, what's yer name agin?"

"Harriman Hickenlooper."

"Harriman Hickenlooper. Where're ya from? Oh, yeah. Iowa."

"Pleased to meet you, Ma'am." Harriman tipped his hat. "This is Rufus Dewes."

The woman didn't acknowledge them.

"Sally don't warm to strangers easy," Jordan said.

He led Hickenlooper into the shack, one big room with a large cooking fireplace at one end, a table and some chairs in the middle and two small beds at the other corner. A musket hung over the fireplace, as did a small tattered Stars and Bars. "Help yerself." Jordan placed a water jug and tin cup on the table and sat across from

Harriman. "Now, why're you really here, Yank? Ain't much to see, an' y'already seen it."

"You ever hear of Eden?"

"In the Holy Book. No, wait a minute. Seem to recall a place called Eden. Don't think it's there no more. What about it?"

"Unfinished business."

"Yer wager." Jordan sipped his water and watched the color bearer. "No."

Rufus shot a questioning look at Harriman.

Harriman motioned to a picture on the mantelpiece. "Who's that?"

"My brother Ezra."

"Where's he?" Rufus asked.

"Out back. Wanna meet him?"

"Yes," Harriman replied.

"Littl'uns, wanna go for a walk?" His children were at his side in a flash.

They walked around the back of the shack. The children stuck close to their father, subdued but watchful in the presence of the two strangers. They crossed a small field and stopped in front of a large oak tree. There in the cracked shadows of its almost barren branches was a small wooden marker on which was crudely etched:

EZRA STILES JORDAN
APRIL 1, 1844 – JUNE 27, 1864

Jordan scratched at his thinning hair. "Back in '61, me, Ez an' 380 other boys from the county volunteered. We called ourselves the Macon County Lincoln Killers." A bitter smile crossed his lips. "Twelve's left. Ez was the good 'un. Ain't a day goes by I don't wonder why I weren't taken instead."

"No, Poppa!" his daughter cried out. She entwined her little arms around his long legs. Jordan clutched her closer.

Harriman took his hat off and gestured for Rufus to do the same. Gazing down at the marker and the little girl, he was moved to reach for Jordan's hand. He found an empty coat sleeve instead and quickly retracted his hand. The girl noticed and looked up at Harriman with something different in her eyes.

"Lost Ez and the paw at The Dead Angle," said Jordan, looking away as he wiped at his eyes with the good hand.

"You whipped us pretty bad that day."

"Lotta good it did."

"I was down the line. Guess we've met before, only we weren't properly introduced," Harriman extended a hand. This time John Jordan extended his remaining hand and they clasped. Footsteps padded up behind them.

"Best you come in now, John," Sally Jordan called. "Supper'll be ready soon. Come, children."

"Where's Ohiowa?" asked the young girl.

"North, far from here, across many mountains, valleys and rivers," Harriman answered. "Best do what your mother says. Say, Mrs. Jordan, have you ever heard of a place called Eden?"

Sally Jordan moved to her husband's side and put her arm around him. She shook her head and guided her husband back to the house without a glance back.

Harriman and Rufus lingered behind. Harriman gazed up into the leafless outstretched limbs of the imposing tree. A shudder ran through him.

"What is it?" Rufus asked.

"That tree. Reminds me of something."

"Care to say?"

"It's why you're here." They sat down under the tree. Harriman closed his eyes. Rufus took out his diary.

CHAPTER 15

"A young boy, he couldn't have been more than fifteen, was captured behind our lines near Macon. The sentries found papers on him, orders, maps, I don't exactly know. The drill was, anyone caught behind lines with documents was a spy, no questions asked. No trial, a rope. Strange thing was, this boy had on a Confederate uniform and freely admitted his guilt. The papers he possessed showed there was a spy at headquarters, we needed to find out who it was, and quick.

"Colonel Granger questioned the boy, explained to him he could get leniency if he would tell the name of his collaborator. The kid wouldn't say who had given him the documents. Granger explained to him that he would hang if he didn't give up the name. The boy still refused. The colonel was upset, knowing what he had to do if the boy didn't back down. The boy gave him no choice.

"The colonel still kept stalling, trying to coax something, anything that would let him spare the boy's life. The more he reached, the more resolved the boy got. We dug a grave by the base of a large oak tree, right before his eyes, blindfolded him, tied his hands behind his back and put him on a horse. The colonel once again pleaded for the boy's life. The boy shook his head. Finally the colonel asked him if he had any last words. The boy said, 'take off the blindfold, please'."

Rufus looked up from his writing and pondered the woods nearby, then Harriman staring at him. "Gosh."

"What I saw in him was something like joy. The boy looked at each and every one of us drawn up in the circle around him. It shook me up, someone that young could yearn to die so sure, so at peace with himself. He settled on Granger last. The colonel couldn't find the words to execute his orders and it was the only time I ever saw him unable to meet another's gaze. We sat tense in our saddles, waiting for a cue from the colonel. I remember the branches above us swaying and creaking in the breeze, it sounded like someone cracking their knuckles. The boy said a short silent prayer. Granger bowed his head and made us all do it as well. Before we could finish, the boy jammed his spurs into this horse, shouting out 'hurrah for the Confederacy!' The horse bolted, the boy dropped off its back, snapping his neck instantly. He twitched once. For a moment the breeze died down and all you heard was the rope twisting against the tree limb. Granger ordered me to cut him down. When I did, I tried not to look into the boy's still open, very dead eyes, but I looked anyway. He was smiling."

"Why, do you think?"

Harriman shook his head. "I've asked myself if I could die like he did. Contented."

"What was the answer?"

Harriman shrugged. "No answer." He rose and headed back to the Jordans' shack.

"Did they ever catch the traitor?" Rufus asked.

"They figured out who it was, but by that time he'd gotten away."

"Scoundrel."

"It doesn't matter. He'll never go home again."

When they returned to the cabin, there was no sign of John Jordan. Sally Jordan was waiting on the porch. "John's restin'. Seein' y'all wore him out." She handed Harriman his walking stick and turned to go back inside. "Told me about yer bet."

As they cleared the Jordans' property, Harriman turned back and saw the little girl watching him through the window. He waved. She closed the curtain quickly.

"I guess the Missus didn't care for us much."

"You think so?" Harriman grinned.

"That's not what I mean. Look what she did! " Rufus pointed to Harriman's flag. "Let's go back and teach her a lesson."

Harriman paused to examine his walking stick. "No."

"You're going to let her get away with that?"

"C'mon."

Rufus wrote in his diary:

"November 24th, 1867

Today we met a Confederate veteran and his family. They live near Macon, Georgia. Nice enough fellow, but his wife was downright nasty. The fellows back home are right. These people have no remorse. This woman had the nerve to sew a piece of a shredded, pathetic Rebel battle flag right onto the flag Mr. Hickenlooper's mother had made for him! I don't know who I'm madder at, the Rebel woman for doing it, or Mr. Hickenlooper for not doing anything about it."

CHAPTER 16

The editor of *The Loyal Citizen* walked over to the Farmers and Mechanics Bank building on the off-chance Ridley was in. It was late afternoon. Connolly figured Ridley observed normal bank hours, which didn't resemble any job he'd ever had. But there was Ridley, hunched over his desk at the back of the room, framed behind the iron bars of the teller's windows. Connolly watched him, steeped in his papers.

Connolly couldn't figure it. Here was a man who could buy any property he wanted. Crop prices were always unstable, and depressed now. Farmers abandoned their farms all the time to find opportunity elsewhere, or just to get out from under debt they could no longer manage. California's gold strikes and cheap land were drawing more and more families west every month. There were many other farms in Appanoose County with better soil and water ripe for the picking. What was so important about Hickenlooper's failing farm? Nothing about this wager made sense. It should never have been made. Connolly chided himself. He had stupidly assumed Ridley knew better than to let it stand.

He knocked on the door. Ridley kept working. Connolly knocked again, louder. Anger flashed across Ridley's face but evaporated when he recognized Connolly. "Hello, Jack. How are you?" he called out, rising from his desk.

"I'm fine, Walter. Is this a bad time?"

"No, not at all. Come, sit down."

Connolly sat across from Ridley. "How is Louise?"

"Just fine, thank you. Sorry, I didn't see you. I'm preparing for a directors meeting this week. What can I do for you?"

"I was curious to get some background on this bet and that Hickenlooper fellow. It won't take a minute. You mind?"

"Not at all."

"You were his commanding officer?"

"Yes. I assumed command of the regiment after Colonel Granger was killed."

"When was that?"

"Uh, that would have been in late November or early December 1864, on our March to Savannah." Ridley eyed Connolly as he made some notes.

"You don't mind, do you?" Connolly asked, pointing at his notepad.

"Of course not. It's your job."

"Granger organized the regiment, correct?"

"We both did. I contributed the money for rifles and uniforms. He recruited."

Ridley thought back to 1861, another lifetime ago. There had been no structure to organize, equip and train the flood of volunteers from every county across the United States that had answered Lincoln's call to arms following the firing on Fort Sumter and the subsequent declaration of war. In fact, there were about sixteen thousand men in the entire U.S. Army when Fort Sumter was fired upon. Except for the small number of men who had fought in the Mexican-American War thirteen years earlier, no one had any combat experience. Moreover, over half of the army's officer corps, many with both West Point training and combat experience, had resigned their commissions to fight for the Confederacy.

Since the army had no system to designate or train officers to lead raw militia units in 1861, it was common practice for communities to elect their commanding officer. Often the wealthiest individuals won that honor, for the simple reason that they paid for the guns and uniforms. It was sheer luck that such men might also be capable of leading men under fire.

An election for commanding officer and staff of the newly-formed Sixth Iowa Volunteer Infantry regiment had been organized. Ridley had not lobbied the men for their votes. He didn't have to. Many of the voters owed his bank money. Ridley was confident enough would vote for him but as he was not a man to leave things to chance, he made sure the vote was done by show of hands, not secret ballot. That way, voters knew he knew where they stood casting their ballots.

Surprisingly, and to Ridley's embarrassment, the initial vote was deadlocked. It looked like another ballot would be necessary, until Harriman and Alonzo Hickenlooper dashed in. When asked who they were voting for, they answered in unison, "Damon Granger."

"Walter?"

"What?"

"I was asking you how you felt about the outcome of the election."

"The people spoke. I did my duty."

"What kind of a soldier was Hickenlooper?"

"Harry? The regiment elected him color bearer after Mission Ridge. It was a distinct honor. And he survived, unlike most color bearers. The Rebels, like us, aimed first for the color bearer. The flag he carried identified the unit. If you could capture that flag, it was the highest honor a unit could attain. Not that he has lived up to it."

"What do you mean?"

"I approved the loan on the Hickenlooper farm. I believed the family was good for their debts and made that clear to my Board.

But the family always struggled. And then the parents died, right in the middle of the war. Harry kind of shut down after he learned of their deaths. And he did strange things. He does strange things. And he is certainly not a responsible property owner."

"What sort of things?"

"This bet is a perfect example. Who in their right mind...?"

Connolly made a note. "Did he have any friends?"

"I never paid attention to that. It would have been imprudent for me to get close to the men. I couldn't be friends one day and order them to die the next."

Connolly nodded. "Of course, but I asked you if he had friends, not if you were friendly to the men."

Ridley flared at the correction, but as fast as his annoyance showed, he covered it. "I would guess that Lucas Rawls is a friend of his. Maybe Jack Burkett. And, of course, his brother Alonzo. By the way, any news of him?"

"Nothing yet. I understand you bought the Hickenlooper note from the bank. Is that usual?"

"The bank was going to foreclose eventually. I saved the bank the trouble and Harriman and me that embarrassment."

"Why would you be embarrassed?"

"I recommended the loan."

"In your view, is there any possible connection between his war experiences and this bet?"

"I can't say that. Desperation. Grief. It could be many things. I really could not tell you. I would encourage you to talk to Harry." He caught himself. "Obviously you can't do that right now." Ridley glanced at a clock on the wall.

"I'm sure you're busy," Connolly said. "If you don't mind, I might return with more questions. For the story I'm writing."

"You're writing a story for the paper?"

"Yes. Thank you, Walter. Convey my best to Louise. And good luck with your annual report. I trust it's been a profitable year." Connolly tipped his hat and left.

"Anytime, Jack. Anytime." Walter Ridley remained seated. He stared at the calendar on the wall and marked an 'X' over that day's date. Only one unmarked day left in November.

As Connolly walked back to his office, he shook his head and smiled. Irma Rutledge was reading when he arrived. "Listen, Mr. Connolly:

"November 30th, 1867

What sense does any of this make? On a crazy wager, a Union man from our town wanders into the Georgia wilderness, making the march he and his gallant comrades made once before. Only now there seem to be more reasons for going, still not clear to this observer.

His reasons hover like ghosts and they whisper questions to this reporter. What happened on this March besides what the history says, or what the fellows recount in their stories? It is becoming clearer to this reporter that there is more to his journey than winning a wager. I hope we discover the reasons if and when he reaches the end of his Second March to the Sea. They will certainly vanish into the mists if he doesn't..."

Irma Rutledge cleared her throat and adjusted her glasses as she finished Rufus' dispatch.

"That's fine, Miss Rutledge. How many more of these are there?" Connolly asked.

"Three or four. He wires something every few days, whenever he can find a telegraph, I would suspect." She looked at him carefully. "It's good, isn't it?"

"Okay, but what's he saying? What's the point?" Several thoughts answered the question all at once. What Connolly saw was a connection between this Second March to the Sea and the national argument about national Reconstruction. "Let me see the others." Might not the wager capture a larger readership than Centerville's and put *The Loyal Citizen* on the national map?

Mrs. Rutledge rubbed her eyes and put her glasses back on. "A one-man peace march."

"Mmm. We won the war, now he's winning the peace... something like that."

"You know, people keep coming up to me, asking how he's doing," Miss Rutledge said.

Connolly nodded. "Is that so?" His mind turned over. The underdog, a bankrupt and bereft Union veteran, on a journey people believed was bound to fail, but which inspired a curiosity to see if he could pull it off, and maybe an admiration for trying.

A one-man peace march.

Connolly knew in his gut that his neighbors, like him, had an ingrained affection for underdogs. It was born out of a struggle for independence from England, the strongest power on earth, homesteading the endless stretches of prairie, fighting Indians and harsh weather, struggling for statehood. Their story, too. The slimmer the underdogs' chances, the more Iowans would root for him! What Connolly especially liked was pitting the "crazy" bankrupt color bearer against the rich banker. Ridley's political ambitions could be affected if, just by a miracle, the color bearer made it back.

Connolly chuckled. He smiled at the notion of Walter Ridley struggling with something he had assumed was a sure thing. And he liked even more the idea of people buying *The Loyal Citizen* to read about it all.

Miss Rutledge was correct. It was one of her annoying habits. The kid could write.

CHAPTER 17

Rufus sat by the side of the road, poring over the map compiled by Orlando Poe, one of Sherman's engineers, done after the March. Every once in a while he grunted and shook his head. "Sixty-thousand Bluebellies make a three hunnerd-mile march in five weeks with nuttin' but the packs on their backs. How'd y'all do that?"

Harriman winced at the boy's attempt at a Southern drawl.

"Come on. I'm practicing."

"For what?"

"I don't know. So I can blend in for the next war?"

"Sounding like that, you'll surely start it."

"Seriously. How did it feel, marching through the heart of enemy territory with no supplies, surrounded by Rebs and hostile civilians?"

"Truth is, we were excited. We hoped the March would shorten the war. But we knew if we could cut through the heart of the Confederacy, we'd be helping get Lincoln re-elected, and that would win the war. If our Lincoln won a second term, there was no other outcome but crushing the rebellion once and for all."

"Unconditional surrender, as General Grant put it."

"Yup."

"Corporal Hickenlooper, what was it like seeing the elephant?"

"Not great."

"How come?"

"Let's keep walking."

"Good idea. It's already December."

CHAPTER 18

"Seeing the elephant, hunh?

It was a Sunday morning in early April. We'd crossed into Tennessee on large paddle-wheeled steamers days before. I remember waking up to the usual welcome smell of coffee brewing and the sound of Sunday prayers being offered. The first rays of sunlight were breaking through the trees, which were just beginning to bloom. I'd heard it was warm in Tennessee in April, but there was still frost on the ground. It was cold enough to hate getting out of bed. Anyway, boys're groaning, stretching, complaining, coffee cans scrubbed and filled, fires being stoked. It looked like just another day on our supposed invasion of Tennessee."

"Why supposed?"

"Since we'd arrived in Tennessee, not a shot had been fired. All the way down from Illinois, boys were making bets how fast the Rebels would run when Ulysses Grant showed up. Remember, he'd already captured an entire army."

"At Fort Donelson."

"That's right. General Sherman assured us the closest Rebels were fifteen miles away. But the patrols we'd been sending out said something different. There were many signs of large troop movements on our flanks and front. Just the night before, our sentries reported the clatter of canteens and wagon wheels for hours in the darkness in front of our lines. I know, because I was on guard duty that night. I heard them, and reported it. Well, Uncle Billy, he was our division commander back then, he knew best.

"This young private, never forgot his name. Owen Buckmaster. Owen Buckmaster, he poured a cup and offered it to Alonzo, who was already up and about. 'Give it to my younger brother there. He needs it more'n me,' Alonzo said.

"'You sure? First cup's good luck, sir,' Buckmaster said.

"Alonzo steered the coffee my way.

"'Whaddya make of it? We been chasin' the Rebs all the way from Missouri. Think they'll fight?' Buckmaster asked.

"'Last I looked, we were in Tennessee, right?' Alonzo replied.

"'Yeah?'

"'So if a pack of Rebs was runnin' around Iowa... Where you from?'

"'Des Moines, sir.'

"'Quit calling me sir. So if'n a pack of Rebels was marching on Des Moines, would you be offerin' them fresh coffee?'

"'Course not. It's just all we do is march, make camp, strike camp, march. I ain't seen one Reb. Not a one. I'd hate to come this far and have it be over 'fore I get a lick in.'

"'If you're so worried this thing's gonna be over that quick, why'd you sign up for three years? I asked him.

"'D'you hear that? Sounds like bees. I get real sick if'n I get stung...'

"A bee hit Buckmaster and his head exploded, splashing his brains all over me and into my cup of coffee. You okay there?"

Rufus flinched. He nodded gamely. "Go on."

"From the woods came a sound I'd never heard before, something between a hog call and an Indian war whoop. I looked toward the forest, and rabbits and squirrels were just hightailing out of there.

That's when I saw the line of butternut men loping out of the trees, not two hundred yards from me.

"The butternuts fired another volley and that prayer group disintegrated before God. I heard more bees whizzing by my head and dove back into my tent. More bees tore into the tent as I groped for my gear. All around me, men were screaming and running in all directions as more volleys crashed into them. Officers tried to organize a defense, but we were green—most of us had never been under fire before. And that horrible yell was way too close. They'd come on fast, like they'd been shot out of the woods.

"Nobody ever knows what they'll do the first time they're shot at. Really there's only two choices. Either stand and fight, or run.

"I ran. Ran smack dab into an officer. He had shaved half his face nice and neat and still had lather on the other half. He grabbed me and raised the broad end of his sword. 'You coward!' he screamed. A bullet tore into him, spun him around, and he collapsed on top of me.

"I got up and ran. It seemed like I ran for miles. I don't think I looked back once. The gunfire got fainter. I got to the edge of a clearing, and that's where I ran into Colonel Granger with a few other men, including Lucas and my brother Alonzo. I was so glad to see my brother. First thing he did, he laughed in my face.

"'The hell's so dang funny?'

"'You got no pants or shoes!' He looked down. 'An you've gone an' wet yerself,' he whispered.

"'What's your name?' Colonel Granger snapped.

"'Hickenlooper. The Rebs, sir, they came out of nowhere and were on us before we could do anything. I…'

"Colonel Granger got right in my face. 'Can you swim?'

"'Excuse me, sir?'

"'I asked you if you could swim.'

"'Er, no, sir. What does that…'

"'Then you have two ways to die right now. You can fight with me here, or you can drown, because you're going to run right into the Tennessee River. Boys, it won't get any closer, we're going to hold here, or die trying." Granger called out, raising a sword and driving its point in the ground. "There's no one else to keep them from rolling up the right flank of this whole army but us. If we don't hold them, except Mr. Hickenlooper here, we will have to swim home.'

"I felt ashamed, I guess, but that infernal Rebel yell was getting closer. 'Yes, sir, we're with you, sir!'

"'Then get your rifles and form up. Hickenlooper, if you can find some shoes and pants, that would be an added benefit.' Granger cracked me a small grin, then went off to collar more strays and form a line against the Rebels, who were now coming on in plain sight. I relieved a dead soldier of his rifle and shoes and went to where Granger had rallied more Iowans and was forming them into a firing line.

"'Hold your fire until I give you the order. Aim low. Load slowly, it will keep you from jamming your weapons.'

"I could see the butternuts clearly now, moving through the field like a dusky wave, cutting a swath through the tall grass, shouting and waving their hats. Granger pulled out his revolver and cocked it. 'Sixth Iowa. READY.'

"I singled out a large Rebel. I remember him because he had the bushiest red beard I ever saw, like birds could nest in it. He was screaming as he ran, with this crazy grin on his face.

"'AIM.'

"The Rebel battle line, smelling blood, ran faster. I thought I was going to piss myself again. 'For your family, for Iowa and for the Union…

"'FIRE!' Our rifles erupted and the entire Rebel front line disappeared.

"But I didn't fire. I was fixed on that big Reb with the red beard. He somehow survived our first volley. He looked around and saw most of his companions were down all around him, and still he kept coming. He raised his rifle and fired. The bullet smacked into the tree next to Granger. Granger said, 'I suggest you fire now, son!'

"I pulled the trigger and the rifle bucked in my arms. I saw a puff of dust billow off that Rebel's chest and he got jerked off his feet, like someone had yanked him backward with a rope. He lay still in the grass, not fifty feet from me. Then his feet twitched and I bent over and retched. A bullet thudded into the tree trunk right where my head'd been a second before."

"Geez!" Rufus exclaimed. "You sure were lucky."

"'Now reload and do it again.' Granger put a hand on my shoulder and continued to fire his revolver slowly and steadily. 'It gets easier.'

"We fought until the sun went down. Load, fire, re-form, load, fire, reform. You bite off enough cartridges, the gunpowder in your mouth turns into a paste you can't wash away. We ran out of water. You couldn't talk, you croaked. We fell back, but we never broke." Harriman's voice trailed off.

"So the first time you saw the elephant, you ran? I mean, retreated," Rufus asked.

"You said it right. I ran, just like those rabbits the Rebs flushed out of the woods. Guess that makes me a coward. But Colonel Granger was right. It got easier to kill. The Rebs never pushed us into the river. Just as well. I wouldn't of made it. I couldn't swim."

Rufus got it all down in his notebook.

Harriman chuckled. "Still can't."

CHAPTER 19

The two travelers approached a white gate fronting a long tree-lined lane, announcing the entrance to a plantation. A graying black man struggled with two large sacks in front of the gate, dragging the sacks a few steps, then stopping, a noticeable limp in his gait. He stared intently at the ground, as if drawing strength from the earth itself.

Harriman approached. "Can I help you with that?" he asked.

The man looked up at him as if he was seeing a visitor from a far corner of the universe.

Rufus recoiled when he saw the man's face. A scar plied it from one eyelid to below his mouth, giving him a perpetual wink and a smile that looked like a grimace.

"Maybe he can't hear or something," Rufus said.

The slave did not answer. It was clear he did not know how to respond to an offer for help, not from a white man.

"Excuse me. Do you need a hand?"

"He doesn't need any help, Mr. Hickenlooper. Let's move on."

Harriman and Rufus passed the man, who spotted the walking stick Harriman carried.

"'Bliged if you would, suh."

Harriman turned around and lifted one of the bags. "What have you got in here, rocks? Is this where you're going?"

The man nodded. "This be home."

"Why don't you be useful?" Harriman handed one sack to Rufus and took the other from the old man.

"No need. I'll take it."

"No, he'll take it."

"That's his job," Rufus complained.

"Take it."

Rufus knew when to stop arguing. "Yes, sir."

They headed down the rutted carriageway, Harriman and Rufus walking ahead, the old man trailing behind.

The sound of hoof beats signaled a large group of mounted men coming up behind them. A moment later, a Union cavalry patrol thundered through the gates and galloped past, coating them in a fine red dust.

"How far is it to Griswoldsville?" Harriman asked.

"Ain't nuttin' there no more, suh."

"How far, you think?"

"Hunh. Depends how you gettin' dere."

"Just like this."

"Hunh. A good three days, I'd say."

Up ahead, the patrol trotted their way. A wiry officer halted the patrol. He noted Harriman's dirty uniform and the flag on his walking stick. "What's your business here? You AWOL, soldier?"

"I'm walking."

"Don't be impertinent. Answer my question."

"I've mustered out. I'm walking to Savannah."

"Why?"

"To win a wager I could get there again, unharmed."

"You been there before, eh?"

Harriman nodded.

The officer surveyed the group. It was definitely not worth the officer's time to get involved with a deranged veteran carrying an unfinished American flag, accompanied by a kid and an old slave. He'd seen stranger sights already, most not nearly as benign.

"I guess once wasn't enough. Be aware there's a curfew in effect after dark." He spurred the patrol on.

Harriman wiped the dust from his sweaty face and turned to the old man. "What's your name?" he asked.

"I be Jed."

"I'm Harriman. This is Rufus. Come ahead, then. I don't like you watching my back."

As they passed around a bend in the rutted track, they could see a large white house framed by the outstretched limbs of massive oak trees, its ornate Grecian pillars holding up a whitewashed brick facade. A porch wrapped around the ground floor of the house. A white picket fence bordering the front yard had long since surrendered large sections to foraging Yankee campfires during the March. The chimney was collapsing. Broad, cracked stairs led up to a wide covered verandah with a few chairs leaning haphazardly against the wall. Black smoke had stained the pillars.

"If ya be so kind to wait here, I go tell de massah."

"Okay," said Harriman, dropping the sack by the steps.

"Sure he'd like to meet ya." The old man met Harriman's gaze for the first time, his eyes pleading. "Don't have many folks comin' roun' dese days, 'cept for the horse soldiers. Won't be a minute." He hobbled up the steps without waiting for a response.

Burton Ball had been studying his accounts all morning and what he saw looked good, on paper. Culloden was more than making ends meet, which was better than what most of his planter friends were experiencing. Some of them had walked away from their plantations even if Sherman had left them standing. They had abandoned their plantations for one reason: they could not possibly do what their slaves had done for generations, the hard work. Devastated by the loss of their free slave labor, planters who knew nothing about hard work and what their slaves had done for them for generations had no clue about surviving once their slaves left them, lured by the federal government's promises of "forty acres and a mule" and the right to a vote.

Ball had held onto almost all his slaves, due in large part because Jed kept things together. More than once, he'd overheard Jed dissuade a young slave from leaving by telling him how much more difficult life was out on the streets, begging for food and work, when all was provided for them right here at Culloden. Based on the numbers, Ball was even thinking he might be able to acquire some of his neighbors' lands at very favorable prices.

Outside, Harriman sat on the steps, listening to the birds. He gazed at the tops of the trees bordering the front lawn. They swayed in the gentle breeze, an undulating golden and red canopy.

"Did you see a lot of places like this?" Rufus inquired.

"Yeah. They all looked the same to me then. Still do."

"Care to elaborate?" Rufus responded, pulling out his notebook.

"Da massa see you now," said Jed, appearing in the front doorway.

Harriman and Rufus walked up the steps into a bare study, a token remnant of books on the shelves.

Burton Ball leaned back precariously in his chair.

"Massa, dis be Mistah Harriman."

"Come in and sit down. Would some lemonade suit you, Mr. Harriman?"

"Actually, it's Hickenlooper. Harriman's my first name. Water would be fine, thank you."

"How about you?"

"Sure, I'll take one. Rufus Dewes."

"Jed, a lemonade for the lad."

Ball waited until Jed left the room before turning in his chair and offering his hand. "My name is Burton Ball." Ball noted the dusty blue uniform and boots. "What brings you to Culloden? You're not with the occupation forces, are you? They just paid us a visit before you arrived."

"What for?" Harriman asked.

He shrugged. "They offer me federal protection services. From what, I ask them. Then I pay for the privilege of getting no answer. Well, sir, what about you?"

"No, I'm not with the occupation."

"Where are you from, if I may inquire?"

"Iowa."

"My, you have traveled far. Are you a farmer?"

Harriman nodded.

"Surely you haven't come to Georgia to farm!" Ball eyed Harriman through cold, bright blue eyes. "I'm a farmer. Culloden has been my family's farm for a hundred and thirty years."

"That's a long time."

Ball let the chair fall forward. "Long enough to learn a few things." He paused and brushed some dust off his frock coat. "Do you know what I learned when I bought Nigroes?"

Harriman shook his head. "I've never bought a person."

"Of course not. More than looking for strong arms, strong legs or a strong back, more than anything, I learned to look into their eyes. The eyes told me if they would work faithfully or be a problem."

"Run away, you mean," Rufus said.

"No one has ever run away from Culloden," Ball shot back.

Jed entered and served them drinks. "Brought you some ginger root tonic, suh."

"It's surprising so many of your slaves decided to stay," Rufus said.

"For a simple reason. It's so much better to have a roof over your head, food on your table and a purpose for living rather than being free and to go begging on the streets of Savannah. Isn't that right, Jed?"

"Yessuh."

"Why was this place spared?" Rufus asked. "Sherman came right through here."

"What makes you think he spared it? Because it has roof, walls and windows?"

"That's a lot more than what some folks were left with," Harriman said.

"Sherman didn't spare Culloden. He killed its soul."

"Is that what you'd have the Freedmen's Bureau believe?" Rufus asked, glancing up from his notebook. "Judging by the number of slaves you still have working, I'd bet your soul's in pretty good shape, Mr. Ball."

"Leave the betting to me," Harriman interjected.

"What do you know of the Freedmen's Bureau?" Ball asked.

"He reads a lot," Harriman said.

"I also know about Sea Island. You ever hear of Sea Island, Jed?" Rufus turned to Jed, who looked down at the ground, then at Ball.

Ball nodded.

"No, suh," Jed replied.

"Sea Island is a place where Negroes have been given land by the Federal Government to grow their own food, not beg for it. It's where they can ply trades as masons, carpenters, even lawyers. It's where they write their own laws and vote for their own officials. It's freedom, Jed."

Ball smiled. "Freedom. A much-used but often misunderstood word. You know, it's ironic." He sipped his tonic. "There is no freedom for someone like Jed. Here, we know the Negro can't handle freedom because we've taken care of him for a hundred and fifty years. But, truly, he cannot be free in the North either, because y'all feel the same way about him that we do, you just can't admit it and you don't want the responsibility." Ball sipped his drink, his wedding ring tinkling the glass and reverberating in the bare room. He eyed his guests. "You think not? Sherman's army beat no path to freedom."

"Staying here is better?" Rufus retorted.

Ball regarded him contemptuously. "Jed knows where he belongs. Every man needs to know where he belongs. That's a freeing thing, don't you think so, Mr. Hickenloper? What is your final destination, if I may ask?"

"Savannah. I have to find a place called Eden as well. You ever hear of it?"

"No, can't say as I have. Beautiful city, Savannah."

"I've been there."

"I see. What will you be doing in Savannah?"

"If I get there and return home, I will win a wager."

"Wager?"

"That I could get there and back home unharmed by New Year's Day and find a place for a monument to our dead."

Ball leaned back in his chair, eyes narrowing, smiling coldly. "Now why would you do a thing like that? I mean, there must be plenty of places for that, back where you belong."

"That's what makes a horse race, I guess. We should be moving on. Thanks for the water."

"Jed, see that Mr. Hickenloper and his young friend get on their way properly, will you? We wouldn't want you to get lost. I hope you find what you're looking for, Mr. Hickenloper." Ball did not rise, but turned back to the view through his bay window, leaning back on the spindly legs of his chair.

Jed escorted Harriman and Rufus out. "I put some food an' water in your packs."

"Thank you, Jed," Harriman said.

"S'cuse me for aksin', but where is Sea Island?"

"Off the coast of Georgia, north of Savannah," Rufus answered. "Why don't you go there, Jed? You could be free and start a new life." He spoke softly, but eagerly.

Jed grimaced a smile. "Culloden what I know. Best I live out what I know in peace. Thass free enough fo' me."

"Well said, Jed." Ball said, looking down from the top of the steps.

"Take care, Jed," Harriman said.

"De Good Lord do that. For whatever you got to do here, may He do the same fo' you."

The two travelers made their way down the rutted carriageway to the road.

"Come, Jed," Ball ordered.

"Yes, massuh."

CHAPTER 20

⸺·◈◈◈·⸺

L ater, after they had walked all day, Harriman made a bed of soft pine needles and stretched out. Rufus made a fire and wrote in his journal. They ate some of the apples Jed had given them.

"Mr. Hickenlooper, what is Eden? Why did you ask about it?"

"It's a place nobody's heard of."

Harriman wasn't surprised that most people had not heard of the place. He figured it had probably been burned. Or maybe people were lying to him about not knowing. Maybe they were angry at his appearance, or his reason for being there, or maybe they just did not want to be bothered. Federal armies enforced martial law. It was an occupied zone. People did not want to be bothered with him. Folks minded their own business and focused on getting by, one day at a time.

The sound of running water interrupted Harriman's thoughts and he followed it to a small stream. He filled his old canteen, drank deeply, refilled it. The day had been warm for Georgia this time of year. He lay on the ground and closed his eyes...

It was their way each day to go on small adventures between the time they finished school and before they had to complete their evening chores. They would wander through fields high with corn or scoot Indian-style through groves of trees laced with undergrowth, which they would hide in and then spring onto each other in a twisting mass of arms and legs and cackles. Often they walked in silence for what seemed like hours, drifting through their private thoughts as they meandered home, without feeling a need to fill up the silence.

On this particular day they had walked like they always did, pushing and chasing each other. Occasionally one asked the other what he was thinking, and usually the answer was "ah, nothing." Fact was, everything was on their minds, the world unfolding before their eyes, the mysterious unmarked paths that lay ahead of them, in the forest and in their lives.

They reached a clearing. Alonzo froze as he caught sight of something there.

"What's the matter?" Harriman asked, and turned to see what had caught his brother's eye.

There, in the middle of the clearing, legs stiffly raised to the sky, a dead calf lay on her back in the grass. Several vultures were tearing scarlet holes in her belly, pulling out strings of red gore. One vulture had picked the calf's eye out and was hopping away with it while dodging the pecks and squawks of the others.

"C'mon, Alonzo. It's just a dead cow. What's the matter, big brother, sight of blood got you?"

"Shut up!" Alonzo wheeled on Harriman, then turned away and retched in the grass. He dropped to his knees, spitting out vomit. Harriman reached out a hand. "Leave me alone!" Alonzo sprinted for the woods, through low-lying branches and thorn bushes that tore at him. Harriman only caught up because Alonzo tripped on a tree root. Alonzo lay on the ground, sobbing.

Harriman sat down beside him and waited until his crying subsided. "C'mon, what is it?" he asked finally.

Alonzo turned over. "I look out for you, right?"

"Sure enough."

"Something 'bout that poor calf, all alone and dyin' and the buzzards pickin' her bones..."

"I don't understand. She was already dead."

"Let's swear right here and now we'll always watch out for each other!"

Harriman rested his hand on Alonzo's shoulder. "Sure I will."

"You swear?"

"I swear."

"Good. I do, too." Alonzo sniffled, wiped his nose on his sleeve and smiled gamely up at his brother. He reached out a hand to shake on it. When Harriman grasped it, Alonzo pulled him down and sprang to his feet in one swift move. Breaking into a sprint, he shouted over his shoulder, "Last one home's a blue-nosed gopher!"

Alonzo was always first—swinging off a low-hanging branch into a chilled river in spring, confronting a schoolyard bully intimidating the class weakling, spending the night in old man Bundt's haunted house. And yes, reaching home after a bad dream on a beautiful sunny afternoon.

Harriman started to run after him, then stopped. He watched his brother cut a swath through a field of corn. He had never seen Alonzo scared like that before, and it shook him.

Rufus called out. "We better get going, Mr. Hickenlooper. Do you want to look at the calendar?"

"I believe you."

CHAPTER 21

Lucas Rawls knocked on the door of the green and yellow Victorian mansion at the corner of Bryant Street. He caught a glimpse of someone peering at him from behind lace curtains. Then the door opened and a sour-faced woman appeared, her black hair tied back in a severe bun.

"Yes? What is it?" she demanded.

"Hello, Mrs. Ridley. I'm Lucas Rawls. Is the colonel at home?"

"I know who you are. Mr. Ridley is busy just now. What is your business with him?"

"No offense, but it's personal, ma'am."

The woman did not move from the door, nor did she open it any further.

"Who is it, Louise?" Ridley's voice echoed from inside.

"One of your soldiers, Walter. He says it's personal." She said it as if Lucas was guilty of something. Louise Ridley withdrew, leaving the door ajar. Ridley appeared behind it. "Good evening, Lucas. What can I do for you?"

"Sorry to bother you, Colonel."

"It's never a bother when one of my boys calls. What's on your mind?"

"Well, sir, it's Harriman Hickenlooper."

"What about him?"

"He's left."

"So? Come inside, Corporal." Ridley shook hands and guided Rawls into an ornate drawing room. The house smelled of hot food and a roaring fire, but the room's salient feature was the number of clocks perched on every flat surface in it. The colonel saw Rawls' awe at his house and furnishings. "Would you care for a drink, Lucas?"

"Oh, no, thank you, sir." An awkward silence ensued. "Colonel, I ain't superstitious, but I got this bad feeling."

"I can see why you would. What he's doing isn't rational."

"I know Har probly better'n anyone alive. He just ain't right."

"I know that. Everyone knows that. What are you trying to say, Corporal?"

Lucas stared at the floor, then met Ridley's gaze. "I jes' feel he ain't coming back."

"I would think you'd hope he made it back. You're his friend, aren't you?"

Lucas looked intently at Ridley. "Sir, all Har has left is that farm. Losin' it would likely kill him. Maybe, just maybe, he makes it back. If that happens, maybe you'd call it off."

"Corporal, the wager will kill him faster than losing the farm ever will. He made the wager, I didn't. Besides, I don't think you're right. I don't think he cares about that farm. The way he neglects it, that farm is a disgrace to his family and himself. Do you know he didn't even plant this year? Do you know that he's behind on his payments? This is not a man who cares much about the only thing he has left."

Lucas shook his head. "But…"

"Some might even say I would be doing him a favor taking it off his hands." Ridley straightened his vest. "I know he's had it rough, but so have you and me. So have all of us. We're all doing what we have to do. Why is he an exception? In any case, it's too late."

Ridley went over to a golden clock and carefully repositioned it on the mantel. Turning to Lucas, he stared him down. "No one is more loyal to my men than I am, Corporal Rawls. I commend you for your concern for him. I will pray that he returns safely. But I will not call off the wager." He went to the door and held it open for his visitor. "Excuse me, but I have to prepare for dinner guests. I would ask you to join me, but it's bank business."

Lucas stood up hastily. "Oh no, Colonel, please. Thanks for hearin' me out. If you see fit to change your mind, I'd appreciate it." He left.

Ridley unbuttoned his tie and vest, looked at his watch and poured a drink.

"What did he want?" asked Louise Ridley, appearing in the doorway. She crossed to a large grandfather clock and began winding it.

"Careful, Louise. The springs are fragile."

Louise paused, turned the key one more time and placed it in a silver bowl next to the clock. "What did he want, Walter?"

"He wanted me to call off the bet."

"Really? What did you say?"

"I assured him I would let Hickenlooper stay on his farm, even if I won the bet."

"That's charitable of you." She started into the dining room, then turned back. "Would you really?"

"Louise! Evicting a decorated veteran from his land is not good business."

"It is politically sensitive," Louise replied. "But it is his land."

"Not for much longer it isn't."

"What do you mean?"

Ridley grinned. "I persuaded the bank to sell me the note. I bought it last week."

"Walter. When were you going to tell me? It's Daddy's money, too. May he rest in peace."

"I was waiting for the right moment to surprise you."

"You are thoughtful, Walter." Louise Ridley glared at her husband. She was used to letting things go that Ridley said as easily as he made them up.

Walter smiled at her and hopped back into his newspaper. "What's for dinner?"

"Leftovers."

Lucas Rawls crossed the street and got onto his wagon. He was about to snap the reins when something stopped him. He knew better than to snoop around, but the bet had stirred things inside him, things about the colonel, Harriman, memories of their war. Puzzled, he got off his wagon and walked into an alley across the street from the colonel's house. There he watched and waited. An hour later, no guests had come to dinner at the Ridleys. Rawls watched the couple eat in silence, one course after another. Ridley scanned his newspaper. Louise stared off into space or gave instructions to the servant that attended them.

As Lucas rode away, he pondered how much less there was to the colonel than had previously met his eyes.

CHAPTER 22

To the casual observer, the barn was solid and the fencing appeared in good shape, but the porch and windows all looked the worse for wear. A few chickens and pigs roamed around the weedy yard. The wash line was empty, save for one large sheet spattered with what looked like bloodstains on it. A thin tail of gray smoke wafted up from the tilting, cracked chimney. The smell of smoke kindled their hunger, for they had long since eaten all of the apples and bread Jed had given them.

Harriman watched the cabin for a long time, circled it twice, approached the front steps, then retreated. He did not respond when Rufus asked him to explain what he was doing. Finally, he wiped his hands nervously on his pants and started up the steps again.

"What is this place?" Rufus asked for the sixth time.

Harriman wiped his brow, furled the flag around the walking stick and handed it to Rufus. "No questions. Stay here." Rufus looked around apprehensively, then moved away from the porch, out of sight.

Harriman walked up the rickety wooden steps to the door, took a breath and knocked. Harriman knocked again, louder. The door flew open so suddenly he stepped back and almost fell off the porch.

Facing him was a girl of about seventeen, with brown hair hanging almost to her waist and the saddest, most beautiful gray eyes he had ever seen.

"What?" the girl demanded, wiping tears savagely from her face.

Hickenlooper tried to speak, but words failed him.

A frail voice warbled from inside the cabin. "Who's theah?"

"Some bluebelly, Mama."

"What's he want?"

"He cain't talk, so I don' know." The girl kept staring at him. "Well, you gonna say somethin', or be on yer way?"

Harriman took off his hat. "Is this the McWhorter place?"

"What if it is?"

"I've come to see Mrs. McWhorter."

"What fer?"

Harriman rubbed his hands on his overcoat. The movement alarmed her and she stepped back from the door, ready to slam it shut.

"It's about her son."

"They're both dead, so git." The girl tried to slam the door, but Harriman planted a boot in the doorway.

"I'd like to say a few words to your ma. I won't take long, I promise. It's about Ford."

The girl took in a small, sharp breath. She seemed torn, but opened the door wider. She pointed him to a stool in the corner. "Sit there." She backed away from him until she reached the bedroom door. Then she turned and went into the room, leaving the door open. There was a faint metallic click, which he recognized as the sound of a hammer of a pistol being uncocked. He heard two faint voices in the other room, but couldn't tell what they were saying.

He stood up hastily and made for the front door. As he passed the bedroom, he saw the girl slip the small Colt revolver into the pocket of her dress. He grabbed the door handle just as the girl emerged from the bedroom.

"Come in. Be slow and talk quiet."

He hesitated. Their eyes met in a wordless moment of mutual loss, suspicion, and curiosity. He reached into the pocket of his overcoat. The girl's hand went to the gun. He explained quickly, "My name is Harriman Hickenlooper. I brought this. It's for your mother." He held up the oil cloth-wrapped bundle he had kept under his bed.

The girl motioned him to go into the bedroom, then followed him in. Inside the bedroom a candle burned on a bedside table. Harriman squinted in the faint light and saw a frail woman lying on a bed in the corner. He couldn't tell her age, but he could see she was dying. The woman stared at the ceiling, sucking in short, shallow breaths, punctuated by acerbic, rasping coughs. Bloody spittle formed on her lips. Only the eyes that turned to him seemed alive.

"C'mere, into the light. Won't bite," the woman said.

"Momma, this fella says he knows somethin' 'bout Ford."

Harriman took off his hat. "Not, really, ma'am. I only met him once."

"How's that?" the girl asked.

"He gave me these."

Harriman raised the package so the girl could see it, then placed it on the bed. The woman tried to unwrap it. The girl came to her side and opened it for her. Inside were a packet of letters tied together with a string, a leather-bound, dog-eared Bible and a small wrinkled photograph. The girl raised each object into the candlelight. The woman's eyes glistened as she recognized the remnants of her son. When she saw his photograph, she moaned. Her hand fluttered off the bed, trying to touch the picture, and fell back. The girl guided her hand to the picture. Her breathing sped up.

"How'd you get these?" the girl asked.

"I promised him I'd return them. I'm sorry it took so long." Harriman nodded to the woman and left.

Out on the porch, Rufus was playing with a cat furled around his leg, making clucking noises and rubbing his fingers together. "Will you answer my question now?" Rufus asked. "Why are we here?"

"Unfinished business."

"You know these people?" Rufus asked.

"Let's go."

A piercing wail ripped the air. Harriman squeezed his eyes to shut out the sound. The girl cried out again. Harriman rushed inside.

The girl lay sobbing on her mother's chest. Her mother clutched the photograph in her hand. A letter lay beside her. Her dead eyes stared up at the ceiling. There was the barest hint of a smile on her bloody lips.

Harriman stood in the corner and watched. The girl's weeping lapsed into spasmodic sobs.

He waited as long as he could, but had to speak. "Could I help you with your ma?"

The girl looked up, eyes wet and running, surprised he was standing there. "I buried folks before," she sniffled defiantly.

"I have, too."

"Bet ya have."

The girl caressed her mother's naked body with a wet cloth in slow, deliberate strokes, softly humming a tune. She squeezed the cloth slowly, letting every drop fall on pale wrinkled skin. She paused to examine a small black spot on her mother's hip. She had never seen it before and absent-mindedly tried to clean it off. After finishing the bath, she dressed the dead woman.

"Ya kin come in now."

Harriman and Rufus entered, removing their hats.

The woman was dressed in a plain wedding gown. She looked asleep and dreaming, that faint smile still gracing her cracked lips.

"Always said the only time she'd ever wear it again was when Papa came home." The girl stood back from the bed. "She's ready."

They dug a grave in a small family plot by a stream and placed the white-gowned woman in it. It started to rain, first gently, then in torrents. Raindrops clattered against the crunches of their metal spades turning up wet, red earth. When they had dug the hole, the girl clutched the Bible that Harriman had returned, but did not open it. Finally, she handed it to Harriman.

"You read."

Harriman read a verse for the dead. When he finished, he began to cover the hole.

"Wait." The girl put the letters, the Bible and the faded photograph of her brother on her mother's now rain-soaked dress, then motioned for them to continue filling in the grave. The girl bowed her head and closed he eyes. "Momma, may ya find relief from the sadness of this world, and may yer soul be taken safely over to the next one. I promise we'll meet there. You, me, Poppa, Holcomb, Ford, we'll be together again. Sit tight, Momma. Amen."

"Amen," Harriman and Rufus said in unison.

The girl adjusted a crude wooden marker at the head of the grave, then headed back to the farmhouse. When they didn't follow her, she motioned them to come inside.

Harriman stood over the grave in the rain. He felt envy and sadness course through him. At least the girl had been there for her mother.

CHAPTER 23

The Mississippi rain came down sideways, falling on Harriman huddled under a rubber poncho in a trench ankle-deep in muddy water. The Union soldiers on the line knew there would be no assaults on the Vicksburg fortifications that day. Still, they crouched down low whenever they were near the trench parapet. Weeks on the siege lines had taught them that snipers never slept and paid no attention to the weather.

"Mail call!" rang out. Soldiers gathered at a wagon parked safely behind the trenches. Harriman took his letter back to his position in the trench, shielding it as best he could from the rain. To his puzzlement, it was from Reverend Wilbur, the pastor of his church in Centerville, instead of the usual letter from his mother.

"Dear Alonzo and Harriman,

"It pains me to write you, especially since I do not know how you are faring and can only imagine what you have been through. Dear boys, your father and mother have passed on. They were taken by the fever on June 15th and 17th. Boys, I pray you can please see that as a blessing from God, for no two people I know could have lived a day longer without each other than your father

and mother. Pray for them, and know they are safe now in His hands. Be assured as well that I pray you are safe, wherever you may be…"

Harriman stood up, flung off his poncho, mounted the parapet, stretched out his arms to heaven and let out a wail that pierced the steady drumbeat of the rain. It startled everyone, Union and Confederate alike, up and down the picket line. No one dared raise their heads, waiting for a shot from the Rebel lines. None came.

Alonzo and Lucas pulled Harriman down behind the parapet wall.

"You trying to get yourself killed?" Alonzo screamed, clutching his brother close.

Lucas saw the letter, read it and passed it to Alonzo.

Harriman stared vacantly at his brother and at Lucas, unaware of what had just happened

A voice called out from the Rebel lines not fifty yards away. "Sumbody tell that sumbitch to screw his head on, else he gonna get it shot off."

"I'll tell him, Johnny. Thanks!" Lucas shouted back.

CHAPTER 24

B y evening the rain had stopped falling. They all sat by a roaring fire, staring into its crackling, fragrant mystery, a deep red glow bathing the small living room. Harriman felt clean, as though he'd soaked in a mountain stream on a hot afternoon.

Watching the girl heft a black stew pot to a hook by the fire and stir it, his gaze drifted up to her face. The fire that painted it red forged an expression on her, resolute and calm. Its stark beauty overcame him again.

"I appreciate yer returning Ford's things." She turned to him. "But, why're ya here, really?"

"I promised your brother."

"That's it? Where ya come from?"

"Iowa."

"Ya came back here from Iowa just to return my brother's things?"

Rufus answered: "He made a bet he could walk from Atlanta to Savannah and come home again safe."

"Why?"

"To find a suitable place for a monument to my regiment's dead, and to save my farm," Harriman answered.

"How's that?"

"I bet my former commanding officer. If I win, I get my farm back, free and clear. If I lose, he gets it."

"That's it?"

"That's it."

"And this?" She pointed to his walking stick and the little flag attached to it leaning on the door.

"My mother wanted me to have a flag when I went to war. She never finished sewing it. I brought it along in her memory, and for good luck."

"You'll need it." She turned to Rufus. "An' you?"

"I'm writing his story. The Second March to the Sea."

"One was enough, if y'ask me."

"I didn't."

"Hold your tongue, Rufus," Harriman said.

The girl glared at Rufus, and went to the fireplace, stirring the large stewpot. "Ya can put up in the barn fer the night. Most of it's dry."

"I appreciate it."

"There's one hitch."

Harriman waited.

"Show me where Ford died."

"Who's that?" Rufus asked.

"My dear, dumb, dead brother." Her anger and sadness were palpable.

"Why'd you call him dumb?" Rufus asked.

An awkward silence ensued. "Ford went to war, he din't come back. Momma din't come back neither. Last few years been like a slow funeral, watchin' her die inside. Ya didn't give me an answer. You gonna show me where my brother died?"

Harriman went to the door and grasped the rolled-up flag resting against the wall. "Ever since I got home, I keep having the same dream. I'm in a battle, and I see a boy through the smoke. I know who he is now, he's your brother Ford. We're aiming our rifles at each other. But then he smiles at me. I'm confused and hold my fire. But then I can see he's going to kill me, so I shoot and he shoots. I see our bullets collide in mid-air. What're the chances of that? Then I hear a bell ringing and I wake up, crying every time." The fire crackled and a peal of thunder rent the silence in the room. "I'll show you where he died."

Rufus looked up from his diary where he'd been writing Harriman's dream. "Is this part of the march, Mr. Hickenlooper?"

Harriman kept his eyes on the girl. "It is now. C'mon." He stepped outside, then poked his head back in. "You didn't tell me your name."

"No, I didn't." She gazed into the fire. "Lucinda."

"Goodnight, Lucinda."

The smell of damp hay greeted Harriman at the barn door and for an instant brought him back to his farm. He paused and let his eyes adjust to the darkness. He made his way to a ladder and climbed into the hayloft, where he took off his wet clothes and hung them over the railing to dry. Lying in the darkness, he wondered how Lucas was keeping up with the place.

At the other end of the hayloft, Rufus scribbled in his diary:

"December 6th, 1867.

Stopping at this farmhouse was obviously something Harriman intended to do from the beginning, yet he never once mentioned the McWhorter family since our journey began. I worry. Does he have the time to make side trips, given his deadline?

Mr. Hickenlooper came this far to return things of great value to a dying Georgia woman—her dead son's letters, a photograph of him, the Bible he carried. What Mr. Hickenlooper does is surprising, it doesn't make much sense, and he keeps his cards close. But I follow him. What sense does that make?"

CHAPTER 25

"Come in."

Jed opened the door to Burton Ball's study. He clasped his hands nervously and shuffled his feet as he stood across from Ball.

"What is it, Jed?"

"Suh, you been very good to me."

"Thank you. You've earned it, Jed."

"An' I knows what it takes to keep the place goin'."

"You can be proud that you are a very important part of making sure it does, Jed."

"Thank you, suh. I been thinkin' 'bout what that Northern boy said th' other day." He flicked a nervous glance at Ball, who showed no reaction. "Suh, I been thinkin, mebbe I best see fer mysef about that Sea Island place."

Ball smiled at the old slave. "That's a long way from here, Jed. Tell me, what is the farthest you have ever been from Culloden?" It was a rhetorical question, and they both knew it.

"Not far. Born in So' Carolina. Bin here ever since, pretty much, 'cep for when I was at Massa Johnson's place in Statesboro. A'fore you."

"You're not getting any younger."

"Got that right, Massa."

"You've worked hard and earned the right to see for yourself. I warn you, though, there may not be a place for you when you come back, as I believe you will. Several young bucks here would be happy to take your place. We both know who they are."

"Jes as you say, I ain't gettin' no younger. So mebbe if'n I don' go now, I ain't goin'."

"You do what you think is right, Jed. With the recent unpleasantness over, the law says you are a free man."

Jed grimaced a slight smile. "Dat's the law. D'you mean it, too?"

"I do."

"I truly 'preciates it, to git your blessing. I'd never sneak out on you."

"I know you wouldn't. When would you leave?"

"Tomorrer, I figger."

"So soon?"

"Truth is, I din't think so, neither. That Northern boy got me thinkin', I s'pose."

"Had you been thinking about leaving?" Ball's anger rose. "Is that all?"

"Suh, ya been good to me, but I got's to go and wants yo' blessin'. Ya knows that. I been here a long time. Ya knows that, too." Jed backed up to the door and out of the room.

Burton Ball eyed his foreman crossing the lawn and knew it was true. No point in making a scene about it. He'd find someone else to take his place. His rage burned for a moment, but it was tinged with regret, then moved into a sudden sadness. Jed had been here for Ball's father. Ball himself had sold one of Jed's 'wives' and two of his children. Jed had done all that was asked of him, and more, and now he intended to go, a free man.

Ball took a bottle of whisky from a drawer and poured a shot. He drained it and dipped into another.

CHAPTER 26

The rain had soaked him to the bone. Red didn't mind being wet nearly as much as the two Yankee cavalrymen at the other end of the bar.

"It always rains when we patrol," the younger trooper whined.

His counterpart, an older man sporting three stripes on his sleeve and the eyes of someone older than his years, ignored him and nursed his drink.

"Last week, same thing." The young soldier shook his head as he surveyed the other patrons in the place. "Raw deal."

"Quit yer whining," the sergeant said. "At least you're on a horse and not walking. Just think about that crazy man."

"Who'd wanna do a thing like that?"

"He obviously has his reasons."

"But walkin' from Atlanta to Savannah on a bet?"

"Listen, kid, if the man made the March to the Sea with Sherman, he's got his reasons. Ain't our concern."

Red walked over. They instinctively put hands on their pistols. Red raised his hands reassuringly. "Excuse me for interruptin', but you said somethin' about a bet?"

"Not your concern either. Who're you?" The sergeant kept his hand on his holster.

"Nobody. Just overheard yer conversation."

"Not only that, Sarge. Did you see, he was carryin' the nigger's load."

"You're out pretty late," the sergeant said. "Curfew's almost on."

"Jus' leavin', Sergeant. Curious. Where'd you see this feller?"

"Two of 'em, a Yankee vet and a kid," the soldier answered. "Ball plantation on the Macon-Dudley road yesterday."

"Mr. Ball, he got any work, you figger?"

"Seeing how many slaves workin' there, it's an even bet," the soldier replied.

"Thanks."

"C'mon, pup," the sergeant said.

The younger soldier finished his drink and reached into his pocket. The sergeant held his arm. "Unh-unh. They owe us a lot more'n this rotgut whiskey." He turned to Red. "You go on home. Wouldn't want to run into you after curfew."

They shoved past him and left.

Red stared into his glass. "This Yank, the one they was talkin' about, d'you hear about him?"

The bartender wiped the bar, then spat into a brass spittoon.

"Yup, sumbody else saw him, too."

"He makin' a point? Yanks already made their point."

"It's a bet, right? He's doin' it for the money. Who knows? I stopped tryin' to figger out why people do things. Got enough to worry about."

"Amen. Say, you hear of any work, I'll be by agin next week."

"Get in line, friend."

"Yeah." Red threw a coin on the bar, tipped his hat to the bartender and hitched up his collar. The whiskey warmed him inside as he stepped out into the night air. It would last long enough to get him home. It had to. He had tossed his last coin on the bar.

The bartender knew it, too.

CHAPTER 27

L ight squeezed through the cracks in the barn walls. A rooster crowed, rustling its hens into the yard outside. Harriman heard Rufus snorting and tossing in the straw in a corner of the hayloft. He had to hand it to the kid. It took guts to come along, and the kid's questions always threw Harriman off balance, as though he was searching for another meaning in anything Harriman said. The kid was too damned curious for his own good. But he knew his stuff, too.

Harriman winced at the acidic pain in his stomach. He dreaded what he had to do. But he'd made a bargain with her. And just as strong as that dread was how resolute she was to go and his desire to accommodate her.

"G'mornin," Rufus said, stretching out.

"Yeah."

Harriman heard the girl talking and peeked out the hayloft door. She had a sack on her back and a broom in her hands and was speaking to her animals, alternately soft, then firm, then reassuring. She swept the porch quickly, efficiently, the cat playfully dodging her sweeps and swiping at strands of straw sticking out whenever she paused. Walking out further into the yard, she swiped at the chickens plucking at the ground.

"Go on, git! Git!" she said, scattering them before her. She walked to the cowpen and led her cows out. Swinging the broom as a bat, she swatted their backsides. "You, too, girls. Git!" The cows protested, but were soon trudging into the woods, their lowing cries trailing off behind them.

"What's she doing?" Rufus asked, watching over Harriman's shoulder.

"Find out soon enough." Harriman descended the loft and stepped out into the yard with Rufus in tow. "Good morning."

"It's mornin', anyway." Lucinda struck a match and set it to the broom. She walked to the barn entrance and stuffed the now flaming broom under a bale of hay just inside the door.

"The hell!" Rufus exclaimed and headed toward the barn. Out came the Colt, aimed at Rufus' head.

"Leave it!"

He froze in his tracks.

She walked back inside the farmhouse and retrieved a large sack that she threw into the yard. Without a pause, she closed the door behind her, descended the steps and crawled under the house, holding the lit broom well away from her as she did. There, she set the broom on the underside of the floor and was crawling back out when she noticed her old rag doll lying half-buried in the dirt. She crawled over to the doll and clutched it to her chest, singing. Cinders were falling all around her, but she lay there, eyes closed, humming.

Springing to life, Harriman raced over to her, grabbed her legs and began pulling her back into the daylight.

"No!" Lucinda kicked out at the hands, but they were clamped on her like leg irons.

He let go of her legs as soon as he pulled her clear. Just as he did, a section of the floor collapsed in a heap of flaming wood. The house creaked and groaned. Flames leaked out of the barn and smoke swirled across the yard. A family of raccoons bolted out from underneath the house.

"Where'd you come from?" Lucinda called after them as they raced away.

"Why are you doing this?" Rufus protested over the crackling fire that was engulfing the entire homestead. Within minutes, the McWhorter house collapsed in a fiery heap.

Lucinda stared at it for a few moments, clutching the rag doll to her chest, gently rocking. Then she nodded, stuffed the doll into her sack and went to the family plot.

The lullaby that came to her was the one that her mother used to sing to her as a child. She closed her eyes and felt her mother's essences again—hard body, soft eyes and a voice that caressed her into sleep. Lucinda sang the lullaby and prayed that her voice would soothe her mother's soul. She saw her mother smile in her mind's eye, and knew at once that she was safe from the despair that had enveloped her. She saw her mother floating away to join her husband and sons. Lucinda knelt and said a prayer. After a few minutes, she turned to Rufus.

"How quick ya kin wipe out a life a' work," she said.

"All the more reason to hold onto it," Rufus replied. "Why are you doing this?"

"No way I'm leaving it to some bloodsucking carpetbagger or greedy neighbor. It's crawlin' with both."

Smoke curled through the porch boards, and she watched it twist high into the sky. It was the very same porch she had stood on with her mother the day her father went to fight with Robert E. Lee.

Her father had been quiet before he left. His bearing had upset her, and when she had asked him why he was so withdrawn, he took her in his arms and held her tight. "Darlin', this world's not comin' to any good." He left for Virginia the next day.

Ford had constantly badgered his mother to let him join his father, but she wouldn't hear of it. Lucinda worried he might run off in the night, and watched him all the more closely. She was split, because she also needed to pay more mind to her mother, who suffered Enoch McWhorter's absence keenly. What Lucinda couldn't know then but understood now was that her father and mother had foreseen the enormity of the death and suffering coming to them all. They must have struggled with their forebodings for weeks. Momma didn't come out of her room for a long time after Enoch left.

From then on, Lucinda watched Momma's moods rise and fall depending on whether a letter arrived from Papa. Some days she was her old self, doing what had to be done unhesitatingly. She would re-read the day's letter several times, then carefully put it into a growing bundle she hid away and focus on her work. Other days, when a letter did not come, she would retreat into her room, not to emerge.

"Why's Momma cryin' so much?" Ford would ask.

"Same reason she don't want you goin' off to the war, silly."

One day Momma received a letter with a photograph of Daddy in his butternut uniform. Somehow he had found enough money to pay a camp photographer. He looked awkward, expressing none of the posturing such pictures often inspired in their subjects. Lucinda beamed with pride when she saw it, but was surprised at the strange look on Momma's face.

A long stretch ensued with no letters. Lucinda started waiting for the postman by the side of the road, lingering longer than her chores could wait, hoping she could be the one to bring Momma the one thing that might brighten her day. Then a neighbor returned home months after Lee had invaded Pennsylvania, bearing a severe limp and something worse. Momma knew just what he had come to say and ran away from the poor man screaming. Ford found Momma lying on the barn floor, curled up in a ball.

It took Momma a year, but she finally began to recover some of her old self. It didn't last long.

Lucinda had been at the stream filling buckets when she heard a scream. She ran back to the farmhouse and saw a band of gray-clad cavalry assembled there. At first she was reassured. Rumors were flying throughout the countryside, warning that Sherman's columns were heading their way burning and looting as they went. Some families had already abandoned their homes and headed further south, while others frantically buried all their valuables and prayed for the best.

She saw Momma run frantically into the clothesline, getting tangled in the drying clothes. "Momma, what's wrong?"

"I wanna go! Let me go!" Ford yelled as he darted between the sheets and pants.

"No," Momma screamed.

"Go? Go where?" Lucinda asked, collaring Ford. "Who're you?" she asked the riders.

"We have been sent to enlist every able-bodied man in the county to come to the defense of our country," said a prim man in a pressed gray officer's uniform.

"Who're you?" Lucinda repeated.

"Colonel Bradford Wheatley, ma'am, Georgia Home Guard." The man smiled and tipped his hat.

"Able-bodied man," she snorted. "He ain't never even shaved yet!" She lunged at Ford, who broke free from Lucinda's grasp and ran back into the clothesline. He got tangled in the wet clothes. Momma dove in after him and held him tight.

The riders watched the scene with bemusement and disdain. "I understand your feelings, ma'am, but every family must do its part," the prim officer said. "The devil and Tecumseh Sherman are coming. To repel him, we must have every man."

"Y'already took my man and my other boy. Lookit him. Ya cain't stop Yankees with boys!" Momma cried. She sobbed and clutched the squirming Ford still closer. "Not my boy."

"I ain't a boy no more. I kin do my duty, Momma, sherly I kin. Lemme go, Momma, please." Ford still tried to wriggle free.

"That's a lad!" Wheatley exclaimed.

"No."

"Ma'am, I have my orders. I will enforce them."

Momma drew a Colt from her dress and with trembling hands aimed it at Wheatley. "Over my dead body."

Ford's eyes grew wide at the long barrel inches from his nose.

"Oh, no," Wheatley said, pulling back on the reins. The horse bucked. The other mounted men looked at each other, unsure of what to do. One of them, a short wiry man wearing a red bandanna around his head, dismounted and walked toward Momma, never taking his eyes off her.

"Don't come any closer!"

"Hundley," Lucinda gasped.

Hundley raised his hands. "Mrs. McWhorter, I don't like this anymore'n you. There ain't a single person I know hasn't lost a dear one." Lucinda heard that peculiar sing-song lilt of his voice, like someone over-acting a lullaby to a baby. "But orders's orders, ma'am, an' if we don't carry 'em out, someone else will. Tomorrer, the day after, but sure enough they will."

"I cain't b'lieve yer in on this, Red Hundley," Lucinda said. She carefully took the pistol from her mother.

Ford ran inside and came back out clutching a small knapsack. He knelt down and looked into his mother's eyes. "I'll be back, Momma, I promise."

Red hoisted him onto the back of his horse. For one instant, Red locked eyes with Lucinda, then had to look away and whipped his horse around. As quickly as they had come, they were gone.

Lucinda gathered her few things and started off. Harriman and Rufus saw there was nothing else to do and followed her. They headed east, toward Griswoldville.

They reached the burned-out ruins of a factory. Further on, they came to a field bordered by stone fences. Harriman walked into the field and motioned for Lucinda to follow.

"I found him here." Harriman pointed to a small hollow. Lucinda watched his face intently, not looking to where he pointed. He felt her gaze on him and moved away. He was surprised to see so many remnants of the battle—buckles, canteens, caps, cartridges—still strewn on the ground, rusting and rotting years later. When he turned, he saw Lucinda drop to her knees. Alarmed, he moved to help her, but realized she had stooped down and picked up something off the ground. She put it in her pocket.

Ford's boyish face wafted up out of the ground, silently pleading with him again to return his things. But Ford McWhorter had been his enemy, and this place hadn't really been a battlefield, but a slaughter pen.

Rufus and Lucinda joined him at one of the stone fences. "So where are we, Mr. Hickenlooper?" Rufus asked, paging through his diary.

"Griswoldville," Harriman replied.

"I've never heard of it."

Harriman walked on, picking his way through the detritus strewn on the brown cold field, pointing as he described what happened. "That was a pistol factory we passed a ways back. Rumor had it someone from Connecticut had set it up before the war. Bad luck, we burned it down. Just as we got to this field, the Rebs came out of those woods over there. We had just taken cover behind that wall. That's where Colonel Granger got killed. I was so angry I was shooting fallen Rebels on the ground. It wasn't really a fight. It was more like murder. Their battle line was bunched together so tight, all we had to do was shoot low, we were bound to hit something. The smoke obscured our view, so we aimed at musket flashes." Harriman started to sweat and feel faint.

"When I saw the boy through a break in the smoke, he was struggling to load a musket. It was taller than he was. The poor kid was watching another man load his rifle, trying to copy him. He spotted me through the smoke. I could have dropped him easily, but I didn't. I just stared at him across that few yards of earth. Standing here now, I still don't understand how anyone could have got close

Antonio Elmaleh | 123

to the wall, especially children and old men. They had muskets and shotguns. We had Spencer repeaters and years of hard fighting behind us. No one made it over the wall."

"He say anything?" Lucinda asked.

Harriman turned to her. "After the fight was over, I heard someone crying out for water. I found Ford lying here and gave him some from my canteen. He was trying to get something from inside his coat, but he couldn't move his arms. I reached in and found letters, a photograph, a small Bible. He pleaded with me to return them to his mother. I didn't know what to say. I knew we'd be back on the march in the morning. I could see he was not long for this world. I didn't want to disappoint him so I promised. He made me swear on his Bible. Just as sure as I once knew I couldn't keep that promise, I've known I've had to ever since." His lips began to quiver.

"What's this?" Lucinda fingered a faded, bloodstained cloth.

"Often we couldn't identify dead people, especially after artillery got them. So boys would write their particulars down and pin them to each other's backs before they went into a fight. That way the gravediggers could identify them and notify their kin. It's how I found you."

"You killed Ford." It was not an accusation, but a statement of fact.

Harriman shifted on his feet. He hated his hands just then. They fidgeted with his coat and plucked at the buttons. He shoved them into his pockets to hide them. His fingers clutched at his legs. "It was him or me." More than anything in the world, he wanted to wrap his wretched hands around her and hold her close. "I'm so sorry, Lucinda."

She pocketed the bloody cloth and took a deep breath, shifting her gaze from where Ford died back to Harriman. She shook her head, trying to make sense of it. "You killed my brother, but you came all this way to return his things. Why?"

"I made a promise."

"Gettin' all this down?" Lucinda turned on Rufus.

Rufus kept writing.

A flash of movement in the tree line caught Harriman's eye. Whatever it was disappeared deeper into the forest.

"The bet says you have to get to Savannah, right?" Lucinda asked.

"And return untouched, before the end of the year. I have one more place to go before Savannah."

"Where's that?" Rufus asked.

"Eden."

Rufus pulled out his map. "Eden, Eden..."

"Ain't gonna find it."

"Why?" Rufus asked.

"Cause y'all burned it down," Lucinda said.

"Hunh."

Rufus moved off to gather souvenirs.

"I wish you and me had met some other way," Harriman said.

"I wanna come with you to Savannah."

Harriman was taken aback. "Sure. Why?"

She stared out over the battlefield, then up into the sky. "East?"

Harriman nodded.

The trio started toward Eden.

CHAPTER 28

A head, Walter Ridley could make out the outline of the Hickenlooper farmhouse nestled against a small bluff along the river. He stopped, dismounted and looked around the farmstead in the soft, unseasonably warm afternoon light.

This was the third time the banker had been out to the farm since the color bearer had set off for Georgia. He didn't exactly know why he came. It wasn't for the pleasure of riding a horse. And it certainly wasn't because he could feel good about satisfying a customer's financial needs. No, coming here soothed a gnawing unease in the pit of his stomach that had begun right after the bet was made, and grew daily. It was something Hickenlooper had said, and he couldn't remember it. Never mind, Walter Ridley felt no compunction about coming unannounced. No one was there. Besides, the place was as good as his.

He dismounted and walked the rest of the way to the farm, making notes of things he would have to fix. The more he saw, the angrier he got. The Hickenlooper farm wasn't an entry on a ledger anymore. He took Hickenlooper's negligence personally now. Still, it bothered him that Hickenlooper had been calm when Ridley informed him that he had bought the note from the bank. If the tables had been turned, he would have done anything and everything he could to avoid something like that happening. No, it was something else, something else Hickenlooper had said that troubled him. Now he remembered. Something about "squaring our accounts." His resentment increased.

"I own you," he reminded himself.

A horse and wagon were tied to a fence railing in front of the house.

"Hello? Anybody there?"

He heard a shuffling from inside. Ridley withdrew a few steps and groped for the pistol he kept in one of his saddlebags.

Then Lucas Rawls emerged from the house, carrying an armful of junk.

"Colonel. What brings you out this way?" Lucas brushed by the banker and threw the junk in the back of the wagon.

"Uh—I was coming back from a meeting in Emmaline and thought I would look in on the place. How come you're here?"

"Har asked me to look after the place while he was gone. I'm doing a little housecleanin'. Amazing what you hold on to long after the need's gone." Rawls went back in the house.

"Things must be in order, then," Ridley called out after Lucas. "It's good to see you are helping your friend. I admire loyalty in a man."

"Least I could do, Colonel. You'd do it too, I'm sure."

"Have you had any word on his progress?"

"Barely nothin'. Just the articles Jack Connolly's been puttin' in the paper from that kid that went with Har."

"Oh, yes, him."

"Ain't it somethin'? Some kid gets it into his head to write a story about Har and the march? At least he ain't dead, or reported as such, right?"

"Well, I best push off. Glad to see you, Corporal."

"Best to the missus, sir."

Ridley mounted his horse and saluted Rawls, who wagged his hand in response and went about his work.

CHAPTER 29

―――――◦◊◦――――

Dispatch of December 10, 1867:

*I watched a man plow his field today. He stooped behind
his half-starved nag with the reins draped around his neck. He
leaned backward against the reins as the plow clawed at the hard
red earth. That's when I saw the empty sleeve pinned against his
side as he struggled to keep the plow blade cutting the earth in a
straight line. He kept to his work, the pale sun catching the sweat
glistening on his face in spite of it being December. He paused once
and held the reins in his teeth while he wiped the sweat off his face
with his remaining arm. Then he was back at it. Occasionally he
would encourage the nag on in a hushed and patient voice. I got
the feeling the nag understood him. I didn't, so I kept my distance
behind the broken fence. And I asked myself, "How can he get by?"*

*What I hear and feel most is silence. And sometimes the feeling
that we're being watched.*

*No music playing, no children laughing. The people talk
amongst themselves like this farmer talked to his horse, hushed
and slow, as if they're always afraid someone might overhear them.*

What secrets do they pass along? Hopes of reviving the Lost Cause? Sometimes I hear the echo of a far-away train whistle. If anyone in the roving hordes of homeless, desperate people hears it, maybe they are reminded that they are not on that train, that wherever that train is bound is better than where they're going, which is nowhere good anytime soon. The darkest secret, but to this reporter, one that gets clearer every day, is that hope slips off, slow and steady, one day at a time, just like a train whistle trailing off in the distance.

Still a few weeks away from Savannah, if all goes well.

"But where's Hickenlooper?" Jack Connolly snapped, looking up from the latest dispatch. "Jeez, kid, who, what, when, where, then maybe, why!"

"Mr. Connolly?" Miss Rutledge set her glasses on the desk.

"What?"

"I like it."

"Why?"

"The pictures of what he sees. He gets me to see them, too. I imagine how frightful it must be to live there. And they remind me of how grateful I am to live here."

"It sounds like you're going soft, like Hickenlooper. How come you care about the 'poor people of Georgia'? I'm sure you wished them all dead a few years ago. I sure did. Goddamn it, we all did! Where the hell is Harriman Hickenlooper! I want details."

"Mr. Connolly, with all due respect. Every day of that war, I dreaded the dispatches, because with them came the casualty lists. Every day I dreaded that I might have to write another obituary, make up something else reassuring to say to a mother for whom words meant nothing. And if I should meet that mother on the street, what would I, what could I say? One day it occurred to me that there must be someone like me in some town in Georgia or Virginia who had to write the same empty obituary, pay the same hollow tribute to someone whose death was just words to them, but meant the end of the world to a mother, sister or wife. I prayed endlessly for God to stop the killing. That's not being soft. That's a fact."

"I'm sorry, Miss Rutledge, I take back what I said. But what's that got to do with Harriman Hickenlooper? The kid won't tell us what he's up to!"

"Why does it matter, Mr. Connolly? You threw him out of your office. You promised him nothing and you're paying him nothing. But you are running his dispatches."

"Never mind. I'll be back at three to go over the rest of tomorrow's edition."

He walked out of the office and down Main Street. Storefronts and houses displayed the first Christmas decorations of the season. Several children nearly collided with him as they threw snowballs at each other. He smelled maple syrup and stews emanating from kitchens as he walked.

Shy, retiring Irma Rutledge, who had worked for him for years, quietly going about her business and usually speaking only when spoken to, Irma had expressed what he saw and felt all around him—mirth and joyful expectation of the holidays—and boundless admiration for how his people endured in the face of all the sacrifices they had born. Even going home to minister what pitifully little he could to his dying wife, all these thoughts filled him with the feeling that there was no place he'd rather be.

There was one thing that bothered him. He realized he was jealous that the kid was writing these pieces, not him. He shuddered at the thought that being bored was worse than getting old.

CHAPTER 30

Red walked down the beech and oak-lined road, fixed on the white-columned plantation at its end. He noticed the blacks silently working in the fields on either side of the road. Some part of him envied that they were working, even though he would never work for free.

Arriving in front of the house, he ascended the steps and knocked on the door. After a moment, it cracked open.

Burton Ball peered out. "Yes?"

"This the Ball place?"

Ball waited.

"Heard there's work."

Ball eyed the stranger up and down. "That would depend on what you can do."

"An' what you need done."

Ball opened the door and motioned Red inside. A distinct unwashed odor wafted in with him. Ball sniffed loudly and left the door open. Red took in the faded opulence that greeted him.

"What's your name?"

"Folks call me Red."

"Where do you live? Where are you from?"

"Here and there. Mostly there. No place like this."

"So, Red, what do you do?"

"Anything."

"Show me your hands."

Red eyed Ball, then offered his hands.

"Turn them over, palms up."

Red complied.

"Did you serve in the late unpleasantness, Red?"

"With Bedford Forrest, then the Home Guard."

"When Sherman came, I take it." He paused. "I assume that you can track?"

Red nodded.

"Maybe you can help with something. Follow me."

They walked into a small room off the spiral staircase. Ball motioned Red into a chair and sat down behind a desk, facing him. "Some days ago, two people showed up here. One was a mustered-out Yankee, the other a teenage boy. They came from Iowa." Ball waited for a reaction. None came. "My lead nigger saw them on the road and brought them to me, saying they were in need of directions. It turns out they were here on a bet."

"Hunh."

"The Yank had been here with Sherman and, according to his story, he had bet he could make the March again."

"Why?"

"I didn't ask."

"And the kid?"

"He said he was writing this Yankee's 'story'. The 'Second March to the Sea,' he called it. I didn't believe a word of it. My suspicions were subsequently proven correct."

"How's that?"

"They stole my lead nigger."

"Why? Niggers're pretty good at leavin' on their own. Law says they can."

"I know that! This nigger has been loyal to me, as he was to my father. There is no way he would leave of his own accord. Why they stole him is of no interest to me. What I do care about, and how you can help me, if we should agree on terms, of course, is to get Jed back."

"This nigger. How much he worth to you?"

"Only if he is returned alive and unharmed," Ball repeated emphatically. "I can't use him hurt. And I surely cannot use him dead."

"How much?"

"Hundred dollars."

"If he's so valuable to ya, why so cheap? My understandin' is niggers're going for a whole lot more'n that."

"Not when they're as old as him. Ninety dollars."

"Greenback dollars? No scrip, no coins."

"Greenback dollars."

"Half now, half when I finish the job."

"I will pay you thirty now, the balance when you have completed the task on the terms I have described."

"And the Yankee? How much to take care a' him?"

"Included. By the way, Mr. Red, what Yankee are you referring to, if you catch my meaning? I will know nothing except that you bring Jed back, and soon. I can't have the others getting ideas if he doesn't return. Are we agreed?"

Red nodded.

"Wait here."

Red looked around the room at a life he could not imagine.

Ball returned and counted out the money.

"What'd you do in the war?" Red asked.

"Defended my home."

"Sure. I mean, where'd you serve?"

"Culloden has been my family's world for a hundred and thirty years. I was here. You would have done the same, I'm sure. Good day, Red."

As Red walked down the tree-lined road, he bridled at what "defended my home" meant. It sounded like some excuse for not fighting. Oh sure, Ball probably fought with his wife or his mistress or to clear a gambling debt made in a drunken card game. But for sure he had never fought Yankees. Red cursed him.

He cursed himself for taking the coward's money.

CHAPTER 31

They stamped out the lingering embers of a fire and bedded down for the night. Lucinda made hers some distance off. Soon the forest was quiet, except for the gurgling of a nearby brook. The moon had risen, casting a silver pallor over the forest floor, the branches of trees creating shadows that undulated in a soft breeze.

At first, it was rustling leaves that caught Harriman's attention. But it was the fire that gave them away, reflecting yellow orbs watching them from the undergrowth. Then the orbs blinked. He heard a short snort, followed by another one nearby.

Quickly and quietly, he roused Rufus.

"Wha—?" Rufus twisted and grunted under the veteran's grasp.

"Be quiet and come with me—now," Harriman hissed, putting a finger to his lips. He crawled over to Lucinda's sleeping form. He touched her lightly on the shoulder. The Colt was up in his face and cocked. "Aim it at them," he whispered, nodding at a circle of dogs that had responded to the lead dog's initial signal and now stood around the campsite, pacing. "Better yet, follow me."

Lucinda saw the dogs and carefully gathered her things, never taking her eyes off them. The dogs sniffed the air and growled, catching the smell of fear coming from the humans.

Harriman scanned the woods. The dogs began to move slowly toward them, stopping and watching, all the while closing the circle. Lucinda followed Harriman with Rufus right behind her. "See that tree?" Harriman said, pointing to a large oak with one thick branch hanging head-high off the ground.

"Yup," they answered in unison, and the three tore off through the brush, briars ripping at their legs.

The dogs were on their heels in a flash. Lucinda reached the branch first and swung herself up, followed by Rufus. Harriman tripped. As he scrambled to his feet and swung himself up on the branch, the lead dog leaped and sank his teeth into Harriman's calf. Harriman screamed and kicked madly at the dog fastened to his leg.

The lead dog held fast, snarling through its mouth. Its cohorts reached the tree and leaped at the frantically kicking color bearer.

Harriman swung back and forth, his body arcing higher and higher, the dog still attached to his leg. Each time he swung, the lead dog smacked into the pack below. The other dogs bit back until the lead dog let go of Harriman's leg to defend itself. Harriman swung himself up onto the branch.

The lead dog was wounded now, overcome by too many other dogs who were furious it had deprived them of a meal. Out of the woods, more dogs descended on the hapless lead dog. It was over quickly. The dogs devoured the lead and circled under the tree, snarling and staring up at the three trembling travelers. Finally, they left.

"I liked dogs once," Harriman said, wincing as he probed his wound.

"I can see why you don't now," Rufus said.

"I don't think so."

"I didn't know dogs ran wild," Rufus asked. "How'd they get loose?"

"Lemme see that leg," Lucinda said.

Harriman drew a breath and dropped to the ground, followed by the others. He rummaged in his sack and found a balm, then washed the wound in the stream before applying it. "On the March, we foraged every day, but each day we got closer to the sea, the pickings got slimmer. The soil was sandier, less fertile. The local people knew we were coming, so they got good at hiding what they needed to hide."

"'Truly," Lucinda said. "Lemme see." She didn't wait for an answer.

"We were always hungry, but our orders were to make fifteen miles a day. It put a lot more pressure on the forage details."

"Why?" Rufus asked.

"They had to go farther from the columns to find food. Remember, we were deep in enemy territory, so anyone the Rebs caught foraging didn't make it back. This one time the detail I was on had searched a plantation and come up empty. We were in a foul mood. And the slaves were acting strange."

"What do you mean, strange?" Rufus asked.

Harriman leaned back, wincing as Lucinda cleaned the wound. "Easy, there."

"Be still."

CHAPTER 32

"We came to a plantation. It looked just like all the other ones we'd come across. And just like the other ones, there was a bunch of slaves at the front of the house, waiting to greet us. They were crying, which was typical. They were weeping because they figured we'd come to set them free. These slaves were gathered in a circle.

"We approached the group of slaves. We saw what got them so upset. What was left of a boy was lying in the middle of the circle. He'd had been torn apart. Alonzo asked an old woman what happened. She said, "Dogs." Her eyes were as dry as a dune.

"It seemed that some slave boys had run off the plantation to join our column. The plantation overseer went after them with dogs. This overseer hated slaves escaping worse than anything, according to the old woman. His dogs had found this one boy and torn him apart. The overseer had brought back the boy's remains and dumped them in the yard for everyone to ponder. One of our officers came over and bitched at us for not foraging. Alonzo told him what had happened. The officer told him to forget about it and follow our orders.

"The slaves opened the circle wider, revealing the dead boy. That smug officer nearly passed out at what he saw. He turned away and retched.

"'I kin fine him what did this,' the old woman said.

"'No time. Get busy, Corporal,' the officer said, wiping his mouth, and stalked off.

"Alonzo waited until the officer left. 'You know where he is?' he asked the woman.

"'Ain't far.'

"'We have no business with this,' I said.

"'Maybe you don't.' Alonzo glared at me. 'Show me,' he ordered the old woman.

"Me, Alonzo and Lucas always worked the forage details as a team, so Lucas and I followed them into the woods. I swear, that old woman could feel the overseer. She'd raise her head, sniff the air, change direction like one of his dogs on the scent of a trail. Suddenly she stopped and pointed.

"We split up and approached a small clearing from three sides. Inside the clearing I spotted a man propped up against a log. He was drinking from a large jug.

"I snuck up behind him. 'Drink up,' I said, as I shoved my pistol into the back of his head. The man spluttered and spit out a mouthful. He reached for a small pistol stuck in his belt, but I laid the barrel of my Colt across his head.

"'Now what?' I asked Alonzo.

"The overseer had this stupid, drunken smile on his face. Then he saw the old woman. Just as soon as his smile disappeared, that old woman broke out in a grin from ear to ear.

"'What're we doing?' Lucas asked.

"'I'm a civilian, an' a Christian man.'

"'Move!'

"When we returned, I spotted a chicken wire enclosure in a corner of the yard. A big red hound snarled and leaped against the wire when he saw us with the overseer.

"Alonzo pushed the overseer into the circle and pointed at the mangled corpse. 'Is this Christian?' he asked. The overseer refused to look. The dog was snarling and barking louder than ever.

"'I had nuthin' to do with this.'

"'That ain't true!' the old woman snapped. To prove it, she raised up her tattered dress. One by one, the other slaves raised pieces of their clothing and revealed a grisly spectacle of teeth marks and the raised welts of bullwhip scars.

"'Is that Christian? You didn't do it?' Alonzo said, pointing at the grisly scars. The man shook his head vehemently. 'Get the dog.' The dog barked even more urgently as two troopers approached its cage.

"Alonzo removed all the cartridges from his pistol except one and handed it to the overseer. 'Here's how it's gonna go. There's one round in that Colt. It's for you or the dog.' He handed the overseer the pistol. The overseer wouldn't take it. The old woman went for it. She would have shot him then and there, but I held her back. We all drew a bead on him. Finally, the overseer took the gun. For a minute no one knew how he'd play it. He started blubbering, snot running down his nose. He crossed himself, stroked the dog's head and fired. The dog squealed and collapsed at his feet. The overseer sat down in the dirt next to the dead dog. You couldn't tell his drunken sobs from the slaves crying over their dead boy.

"'How did you know where to find him?' I asked the old woman.

"'Overseer took me there many times. Many times. I's pretty once.' The old woman gazed at the overseer, the dead dog, the weeping slaves. She said, 'Praise the Lord.'"

Looking up from the notes he'd scratched in the dark, Rufus asked, "Is Georgia full of wild dogs?"

"Folks set 'em loose rather than feed 'em with no food around," Lucinda said.

"Slaves and dogs, set free," Rufus said.

"Wasn't the dogs' fault," Lucinda snapped.

"Tell it to that slave boy," Harriman retorted.

Lucinda covered the dog's carcass with branches and leaves, then went off to sleep.

Diary entry of December 14th, 1867

Something woke me up in the middle of the night. When I looked over, I was shocked to see Mr. Hickenlooper and the girl whispering in what seemed like an embrace. I knew Mr. Hickenlooper really liked her. But I never figured she felt anything like that for him.

When my eyes adjusted to the dark, I could see the Rebel girl was sitting over Mr. Hickenlooper, holding a D-bar knife to his throat. The D-bar was the biggest knife ever made, the same knife soldiers used to carry as a sidearm. Something I always wanted.

I inched a little closer and heard what they were saying. "I don't know what to do. Ya did my family a kindness returning Ford's things to Momma. It helped her go more gentle. But you killed my brother and I hate you for it."

Mr. Hickenlooper stared up at her for the longest time. Then he said, "You do what you think is right." He reached up and held her hand. For a moment, I thought he was going to push down on the handle. He just looked in her eyes and held her hand. Finally, the girl started to cry and dropped the knife. He held her for a moment, then she pulled away and went back to her sleeping place, sobbing.

But what Mr. Hickenlooper did next surprised me even more. He didn't yell at her, or tell her to go. All he said was, "I hope you won't do that again," and went back to sleep.

The next morning he returned the D-bar to her. I wanted that knife.

CHAPTER 33

C aptain Lawrence Jackman squinted through his field glasses, scanning the countryside while his horse pawed the dirt nervously. Today Jackman was leading a patrol of twenty cavalrymen, mostly green recruits and a few veteran non-coms. They had been searching for horsemen who were harassing Negro freedmen working their newly-gotten farms. This particular band was suspected of killing a freedman and his entire family, then leaving their mutilated corpses to rot under burning crosses.

The captain cursed his duty. He had been drafted in the waning days of the war, uprooted away from a lucrative stock speculating job in his father's New Jersey business. Unable to convince his father to pay for a second to replace him in the army, he suffered what was to him the ultimate indignity—he didn't get the chance to kill Rebels. Instead, he was assigned to the pit-hole that was Georgia, where the most he had done for the last year and a half was subdue drunken, disorderly, jobless white trash and jail the occasional curfew violator.

It hadn't escaped Captain Jackman that carpetbaggers exploited anarchy in the South. He had to marvel at the ingenuity and variety of their get-rich schemes hatched to exploit poor white labor, usually ex-soldiers, desperate for a job, any job. At the same time, he resented guarding ignorant slaves at voting places; and freedmen, landowners now because of the government's policy of forty acres and a mule. If they were so entitled to freedom, they could bloody well protect themselves.

Jackman had decided to make the best of the two gold bars on his blue collar. He, with a few of the other officers in his regiment, had begun collecting "fees" under the table, from store owners and planters anxious to guard whatever meager goods and crops they had from marauding bands of desperate ex-Confederate soldiers and the endless hordes of refugees that roamed the countryside. These officers pooled their fees to return home rich men. Their racket soon expanded to confiscating livestock and supplies "off the top" from these very same merchants and planters, and then selling the goods into a black market that flourished in the absence of any functioning legal system. Sometimes they sold the things they stole back to their original owners. What could they do, call the cavalry? He chuckled at the simplicity of it.

Chasing and capturing murderers was different. The possibility of combat, medals and promotion excited him. He might feel more like a soldier and less like a policeman.

"Smoke, two miles east of here," the burly Irish sergeant announced. The sergeant had led a detachment returning from a scout ahead of the main column. Jackman swiveled in his saddle and saw a thin wisp of black smoke curling out of an endless sea of evergreens.

"Right, Sergeant Skilleen. Form a detail of four men. Sergeant Robison, you will remain with the main column while I investigate. If we don't return in an hour, come for us."

"Four, sir?" Skilleen asked. The only advantages these patrols had were numbers and the greater firepower of their repeating rifles. The sergeant did not trust this captain. He recognized recklessness from bitter experience during the war. Still, orders were orders.

Captain Jackman rode the patrol hard. He led his troops across a stream and up an embankment to what had been a small farmstead—

cabin, stock pen and barn—but was now a smoking ruin. A few chickens and pigs wandered aimlessly in the yard.

"Search the place," Jackman ordered.

The detail dismounted and fanned out.

"Place is abandoned, Captain," Skilleen reported after a perfunctory search. "Best to get back, sir."

"Just a minute, Sergeant. Have the men round up the animals. We take the livestock with us. Can't let it go to waste." He watched in amusement as his men chased the terrified animals around the yard. "You're sure no one's here, Sergeant?"

"No sign of anybody sir," Sergeant Skilleen replied.

Red had also seen the smoke. When he arrived at the still-smoldering farmstead of the McWhorters, what he saw was a Union patrol looting it. Holcombe, the oldest McWhorter boy, had been his friend. The only time he remembered crying, other than the day his dog died, was the day he learned Holcombe had been killed at Spotsylvania.

Now Red watched from the woods, counting the Yankee soldiers, and felt a black rage mounting inside him. He snuck up to the sentry guarding the patrol's horses.

"Go, Henry!" The sentry was cackling and slapping his thigh at the spectacle.

Red threw a hand over the sentry's mouth and snapped his neck. After relieving the sentry of his saber, pistol and carbine, he untied the other horses, sent them scurrying into the forest, and got on the sentry's mount.

Leaning on his saddle, Jackman lit a cigar and watched the circus of cavalrymen and protesting pigs running in circles in the yard. The sound of horses galloping into the forest distracted him. He looked up and saw a man's red bandanna and the barrel of a cavalry carbine pointed at him. He felt his chest cave as the bullet knocked him off his horse. Lying on the ground, the last thing he saw was the sky. It swirled into a buzzing white cloud. The last thing he felt was tremendous relief that the cloud sucked him into it.

CHAPTER 34

They paused by the side of the road. Signposts pointed crazily in all directions. One had read "Eden," but someone had scratched it out, replacing it with "RIP, thanks to Yanks."

They walked further.

The bushes nearby rustled slightly, followed by the sound of hushed giggles.

"Who's there?" Harriman called out.

The giggles retreated into the forest.

"Mr. Hickenlooper, let's not go looking for trouble," Rufus said.

"A little late for that. Who's there?" Lucinda called out. She followed the sounds into the trees.

The forest got darker and wilder the farther they searched for the sounds of giggling. When they emerged into a clearing, they found a campsite comprised of a few small lean-tos. A fire-pit ringed by large rocks sent a spindly wisp of smoke into the forest canopy. A rickety-looking treehouse perched overhead. Animal hides hung from branches. A small pine sapling, bedecked with bits of colored cloth, ribbons and tin utensils stood next to the fire-pit. Sitting atop the sapling was a crude, stick-built star.

"Hello?" Lucinda called out.

Rufus circled around, examining the campsite. He glanced up and thought he saw something in the treehouse, but whatever it was ducked down inside. "Hey, I saw someone."

"We ain't gonna hurt you, show yerself," Lucinda said firmly.

More giggles, followed by a shushing noise. A boy of about thirteen finally appeared in the treehouse. He looked like a wild animal, with matted hair, dirty skin and wild eyes staring down on them. "What you want?"

"I'll ask you the same question," Harriman said.

"Ya got any food?"

"What's so funny?" Lucinda asked.

"That flag."

Harriman reached into his pack and pulled out a piece of bread, putting it on one of the rocks by the fire-pit. More children emerged out of nowhere. None approached. Harriman peeled off more pieces and stepped back from the fire pit. The children approached and took the bread, stuffing it in their mouths as they quickly withdrew again.

One child, a small dark-haired girl with deep, sunken eyes, walked up to Harriman's walking stick and stared at it. She reached out and ran her tiny fingers across the fabric. Lucinda came toward her, but the girl suddenly grabbed the stick and ran off with it.

"Don' mind Gracie, she's kookoo. Don't talk, neither," the boy said.

"How come?" Rufus asked.

"Nuthin' to say, I guess."

"Or too much," Lucinda said, and followed her.

"Why're you living like this? Where are your parents?" Rufus asked.

"Dead, gone, don' know. We hunt, fish, got a place to sleep. Caleb and Reuben catchin' us some dinner right now, I hope." He chuckled. "No one to boss us around or beat us, neither."

Harriman walked the campsite, examining the artifacts the children had collected: tin army cooking utensils, pieces of torn clothes, twine, glass. The smallest item one might have thoughtlessly thrown away, the children had saved and used. Harriman noted how capably they had skinned and dried the animal hides.

He followed after Lucinda. He found her sitting close to the mute girl, both of them perched on a log. He watched them from a short distance.

The girl was sewing something onto his flag with intense concentration. Lucinda watched and occasionally commented in low whispers. She saw Harriman and waved him away.

At the campsite, a girl cautiously approached him, twisting strands of her hair through her fingers. "Where're you from, mister?"

"Iowa."

"Where's that?"

"If you went to school, you'd know," Rufus said.

"Up north," another boy spoke up.

"How you know that?" the girl shot back.

"Lookit the blue uniform, stupid."

"Schools? Ain't no schools around here," Lucinda said as she and the girl Gracie returned to the campsite. Gracie was holding the walking stick close to her body, guarding it from the others. Lucinda nodded and the girl handed the walking stick back to Harriman.

Gracie had sewn a piece of Lucinda's rag doll—the one Lucinda had retrieved from under her house—onto his small flag. Harriman was taken with the detail and care she had put into it. "Thanks. It's very nice." The little girl stared at him for a moment, smiled shyly and walked away.

"Guess we should be going," Rufus said.

"An' leave 'em?" Lucinda asked incredulously.

"Or what? Take them to Savannah? What are they going to do there? They wouldn't come, anyway. They like it here. They've made a home. Who's going to catch them? You've herded cats before? Not me. Besides, I'd never make it back to Centerville in time, being responsible for a bunch of kids." When he looked around, as silently as they had appeared, the children had melted away. "What's today, anyway?"

Rufus knew the days by heart. "December 18th."

Harriman gathered his stick and pack. "You going to stay?"

She shook her head and sighed. "No."

"They'll be okay," Rufus said.

"Or they won't. Who'll ever know?" Lucinda replied.

As Harriman passed the spindly Christmas tree, he stopped and pulled a brass button off his coat. He placed it on the stick star sitting on the top of the tree, and straightened the star. Lucinda laid her rag doll at its base, smoothing out its tattered, scorched dress one last time. They turned back to the deserted camp.

"Merry Christmas," Harriman and Lucinda called out, accidentally in unison.

Later that morning, they arrived at the edge of a large field. A stream ran along one end and trailed off to the base of a slope. The land rose up to a white farmhouse perched at its crest. When Harriman saw the house, he stopped in his tracks as if pulled to a halt.

"What?" Rufus asked.

"You stay here," Harriman said.

"Where're you goin'?" Lucinda asked.

"I'll be back in an hour or so. Don't follow me. I'll come for you." His tone signaled no debate. They saw him disappear across the field.

In another corner of that same field, a teenage boy watched them. His friend lay on his back, staring up into the trees. Two long rifled muskets lay in the grass beside them. "We been here all mornin', and got nuthin but some squirrels. Oh, I forgot 'bout the bluejay ya shot fer fun. We better move along an' find another place. Everyone'll be angry. An' hungry."

Reuben Carnes, the red-haired boy, hissed his friend quiet, cupped his hand over his eyes and squinted into the weed-choked field. Then he pointed to a blue-uniformed figure weaving in and out of the weeds, a small Stars and Stripes affixed to his walking stick. "Get a load a' this," he beckoned to his friend.

"What?" Califf Godbey took a swig of moonshine.

"It's a goddamned Yankee, walkin' by hisself," Reuben whispered. "What's he doin'?"

Califf checked his gun. He got next to Reuben and made out the blue figure in the distance. He scanned the surrounding landscape to see if anyone else was around, then raised the rifle to his shoulder.

"What're you doin? Y'ain't gonna shoot 'em!" Reuben exclaimed.

"Who killed yer daddy, remember? Now keep yer voice down, you idiot."

"Sher as shit wasn't this one! Why in hell'd he come back here if'n he did?"

"He's fool enough to strut around where he don' belong, he deserves killin'," Califf spat. "B'sides, a Yankee's a Yankee."

"Ya ain't gonna hit shit with all that moonshine in ya," Reuben chided. "Cain't hit nuthin' sober, neither," he chuckled under his breath.

"Whaddya give me if I do?" Califf asked, weaving unsteadily as he aimed the gun. "Whooo!" He playfully swung the gun around at Reuben, who ducked and fell over backwards. Califf laughed, aimed and fired.

A bee buzzed past Harriman's head. Sweat poured off his forehead as he quickened his pace, his eyes fixed on the farmhouse. Its windows were smashed, its walls scarred by bullets and fire. The roof had caved in. Getting closer, it all came rushing back to him...

CHAPTER 35

"Choose a detail for tomorrow," Walter Ridley said as he stood over maps spread out on a table in his tent.

"Reminding the colonel, Company D foraged yesterday, sir," Alonzo said.

"Take a squad and a wagon. The column should bivouac here by evening." Ridley pointed to a spot on the map. "Any questions?"

The brothers bent down over the map, examining where the colonel had pointed. Harriman made a note of the spot on a piece of paper. "Isn't a squad too small for a foraging party, Colonel?" Harriman asked. "We've been going in larger groups than that."

Ridley glared at Harriman. "Scouts report no Rebels within seven miles. When was the last time we met any organized resistance?" It was a rhetorical question.

Neither brother answered, knowing it was useless to argue with Ridley. They also didn't bother to mention the incessant sniping and harassment foraging parties encountered daily, because he couldn't have cared less. What Ridley said was true. But Confederate cavalry units, and worse, Rebel deserters, had been exacting vicious revenge on foragers who strayed too far from the main columns.

Fresh in their memories was a private they both knew, a seventeen-year-old named Wilson. Hickenlooper had found him tied to a tree, naked and disemboweled, with Sherman's Special Field Order Number 120 stuffed in his mouth. He had been caught "foraging liberally," as the Field Order mandated.

"Besides, you have quite the reputation as two of the best foragers in the regiment. Your compatriots have come to appreciate and anticipate the fruits of your labors. I have two other foraging details going out tomorrow. That's what I can spare for yours. That's all."

"Yes, sir."

Harriman was about to protest, but Alonzo took his brother by the arm and ushered him out of the tent before he could get in trouble.

"Oh, there is one more thing. Close the flap. Bring me a clock, I'm a collector. Bring me a good one. And for God's sake, make sure it is in working order."

"Excuse me?" Harriman asked.

"You heard the colonel, Har," Alonzo interjected, pulling on his brother's arm again. "The colonel wants a clock, so we'll get him a clock."

"I'll pay you," Ridley said.

"How much?" Alonzo asked.

Harriman rolled his eyes.

"Ten dollars."

"Each," Alonzo and Harriman said.

Ridley nodded, annoyed. "Dismissed." He waved them away and returned to his maps.

"He's going to kill us, Alonzo," Harriman fumed as they walked from the tent. "He's just doing it legal."

"C'mon, Har. He just wants a clock. How else's the idiot gonna know what time it is? He's right about one thing: we are the best foragers in the regiment, an' we always come back with somethin' good."

"That's two things." Harriman sighed. "I have a bad feeling about this, Amos."

"Don't call me that. Someone'll hear you. Relax. This war's over, Har. He was right about another thing, an' you'd agree with me. We ain't seen any Reb infantry fer weeks, since the fight at the pistol factory."

"Griswoldville," Harriman added.

"The best they can muster is grandpas and puppy dogs. We'll go for a ride, take our sweet time, hit a few farms and be back for supper. What's the name of that place he said to meet up? Heaven? Paradise? It's perfect."

"Eden," Harriman said glumly. The irony was not lost on him.

"Who should go on this one? Never mind, I'll sort it out. Relax, brother."

Soldiers had noticed that the rich, loamy earth of central Georgia was gradually giving way to sandier soil, a sure sign the army was getting closer to the sea. The foraging parties had to ride in wider and wider arcs to secure the daily needs of an army marching fifteen to twenty miles daily, rain or shine. The foragers risked a greater chance of meeting hostiles eager to send them the way of Private Wilson. If they ran into trouble, there was nobody to help them.

The detail left early in the morning the following day. All day they poked through barns, dug up yards, searched root cellars, and questioned surly residents, all with meager results. The sun was beginning to soften into the last hours of the day. The men were restless to return before it got too dark. Alonzo prodded them on.

As they crossed one more barren field, the man riding scout, a trooper named Burleigh, galloped up. "There's horsemen coming up behind us."

"How many?" Alonzo asked.

"Twenty, maybe twenty-five," Burleigh answered.

"How far back?"

"Two, maybe three miles at most. Ain't sure they're onto us, but they keep comin'. Maybe looking to make trouble for the column, just following us back to it."

"No Rebel presence for seven miles," Harriman said to Alonzo, mocking Ridley's earlier assurance.

Over the next hour, Burleigh reported that the Rebel horsemen had steadily gained on them, even though Alonzo had altered their course. The light was rapidly fading in the western sky.

Alonzo spotted a farmhouse perched on a hill and ordered them to make for it at a gallop. When they reached the house, he dismounted, bounded onto the porch and banged on the door. No one answered. He took out his pistol and banged again with the butt end. A woman cracked the door open and peered out.

"S'cuse me, ma'am. By order of William Sherman, Commanding General of the United States Army of the Tennessee, I hereby requisition this place."

"Yer doin' what?" the woman asked.

"We gotta borrow yer house, ma'am." The woman recoiled at the Colt in his hand. Alonzo lowered it and held it by his side.

The woman's arm jerked. Alonzo looked down and saw a young girl hitched fiercely to her mother's sleeve, eyeing his Colt with wide-eyed dread. He didn't holster the gun. The woman gazed past him and saw the Union detail.

"What fer?" the woman asked.

"I don' have time to explain, ma'am," Alonzo answered. He pushed the woman and her daughter toward the rear of the house. "Crawford, watch them." Alonzo surveyed the interior. "The rest a' you, get the horses in here."

"Come again, Hickenlooper," snapped a short, stocky private named Wilkerson. "I say we get the hell outta here!"

"Wilkerson. Two things. One. I ain't goin' around Georgia in the dark, trying to find the column. Two. I ain't arguin' with you."

"Yer nuts," snarled Wilkerson. "C'mon, boys, don' you see he's..."

"An' three. You're dead if you don't do what I say." Alonzo cocked his revolver and leveled it at Wilkerson's forehead.

"You won't do it. You'll have them Rebs here faster than a fly on shit."

"We're wasting time!" Harriman exclaimed. He steered Wilkerson away and helped him maneuver the horses into the large main room of the house.

"My God, you can't do this," the woman exclaimed, retreating from the horses crowding her living room.

"Settle the horses, Wilkerson," Alonzo barked. "An' tie up their muzzles good."

"Yeah, yeah. Oh, Mr. Commanding Officer, what about them?" Wilkerson pointed over Alonzo's shoulder. Rebel horsemen had stopped at a stream at the base of the hill. They were still unaware of the Yankees. They had dismounted, posted lookouts, filled their canteens, in no rush.

Alonzo watched through his field glasses. "From their looks, they ain't regulars. More like deserters, which is good," Alonzo said. "We just stay quiet an' let 'em pass."

"Why?" Crawford asked.

"You think deserters wanna get in a ruckus and draw enough attention that some of the friends they skedaddled out on catch up with 'em? They risk gettin' caught by their own if they tangle with us. Rebs shoot deserters, too."

"Shit!" Wilkerson cried out.

Alonzo saw the woman bolting down the hill toward the band of horsemen, pulling her daughter frantically behind her, screaming and pointing at the house. "Crawford, you were supposed to watch them, goddamnit!"

"She kicked me in the you-know-whats and hit me over the head. 'Fore I knew it, she was out the door."

"Rebel bitch!" Wilkerson raised his rifle.

"No!" Harriman tried to grab it.

Wilkerson fired. Dust puffed out of her back and the woman pitched forward. Her body kept rolling down the hill. Her daughter chased after her, screaming. Wilkerson levered another round into the chamber and was drawing a bead on the little girl.

"You idiot!" Harriman slammed his rifle butt into the back of Wilkerson's head and grabbed his rifle.

One deserter galloped to the little girl and scooped her up in his arms, then rode back to the others, who were now mounting their horses and forming up.

"We're in it now, boys!" Alonzo said.

"I knew we shoulda run for it when we had the chance!" Burleigh whined.

"Quit yer whinin' and get ready for a fight!" The Yankees frantically piled furniture and anything else they could lay their hands on against the doors and windows.

"Leave the back door uncovered and the window next to it," Alonzo ordered.

"Why?" Harriman asked.

Alonzo tapped his head and winked.

The deserters reached the edge of the farmyard, dismounted and spread out. A man wearing a plumed cocked hat and a short Yankee cavalry jacket barked orders while surveying the farmhouse. "Whoa in there, Yanks! Y'ain't got no call shootin' a woman. Yer surrounded. No other Yanks fer miles around. Give it up and c'mon out, 'fore we kill ya."

"You'll kill us anyway," Harriman yelled back. "Goddamn you, Ridley!" he cursed under his breath as he drew a bead on the deserters' leader.

"No! No shooting unless they rush us!" Alonzo beckoned everyone to him. "We got three advantages—they don't know how many of us're in here, they don' know we got horses and..." He tapped his Spencer. "They don't know about our friends here. We'll wait until dusk. We'll go out the east door, the same direction the column's heading in. On my signal, we'll lay down as much fire we can on anyone on the east side of the house, then make a run for it east. They won't know what hit 'em. We'll go in pairs. Wilkerson, McDowell, then Crawford, Burleigh, then Har an' me. If we're lucky, we're gone 'fore they come to their senses. If you get separated, keep goin' east an' hope you speak good Georgian. If yer unlucky, yer dead, so don' worry about it. An' if you think you're gonna get caught, save a round fer yerself. Clever Wilkerson here shot a woman." He glared at Wilkerson. "Questions?"

No one spoke up.

A clock's chimes rang out from somewhere in the house, breaking the silence.

Alonzo and Harriman exchanged glances. "Keep them horses quiet 'til we make our move," Alonzo said.

"C'mon, Billy. Yer surrounded!" Cocked Hat called out.

"Say, Johnny, what outfit you with?" Alonzo replied.

"Uh, 12th Mississippi cavalry. How 'bout you?" The pause in his reply betrayed him.

"Whyn't you boys just keep ridin'? Sorry about the woman. We got idiots on our side, too. Shootin's sure to bring more of us. Or some of yer own," Alonzo called out.

"Give it up, Billy!"

"Can't do it, Johnny!"

"Yer miles from your column. We'll wait y'out."

"I ain't dyin' in Dogbreath, Georgia, an' I ain't spendin' Christmas in Andersonville, neither!" Alonzo replied.

"Then how 'bout a holiday in hell? Give 'em a toast, boys!" Cocked Hat roared. Several deserters loosed a volley while others dashed up the slope into the front yard. Bullets crashed through windows and buried in the walls.

"Single shots, boys," Alonzo said.

Harriman fired, dropping one deserter. "Goddamn you, Ridley."

"Why'd you keep sayin' that?" Crawford asked from his position at one of the windows.

The deserters fired another volley. There was a muffled neighing and a crash from inside the parlor, then screaming. Harriman ran into the parlor and found Wilkerson desperately trying to extricate himself from beneath a horse that had been shot and collapsed on top of him. The stricken animal kicked out violently, keeping Harriman away from the trapped soldier.

"Jesus, get him off me!" Wilkerson gasped.

Harriman drew his pistol and shot the horse once through the head. He pulled at the dead horse but could not move it.

Wilkerson's face turned bright crimson. He gasped for breath and flung his arms out toward Harriman. His eyes rolled up in his head and he emitted a choked gurgle. White spittle bubbled out of his mouth and he lay still.

The other animals stomped and kicked as more bullets crashed through the glass. They snorted through the cloths tied around their noses. "One down, five left," Harriman muttered, crouching and trying to soothe the horses.

The clock chimed again, making counterpoint with bullets embedding in the walls and horses shying and snorting through their muzzled noses.

"Goddamn you, Ridley." Harriman saw the clock on a mantel and grabbed it.

Califf Carnes rammed another cartridge in his rifle and tried to put the primer cap on, but dropped it. Reuben laughed from his perch atop a nearby rock. His cackle cut off abruptly.

"Dammit!" Califf fumed. He aimed and fired. The flag and flag-bearer kept trundling across the field.

"Shit!" Califf cried, fumbling with another cartridge.

Cold steel nudged the back of his neck.

"Real funny, Reuben."

"Drop the gun," Lucinda demanded.

"Wha—?" Califf craned his neck around.

"I mean it. Drop the gun, else I'll spread yer brains across that field." There was the distinctive sound of a Colt being cocked.

Califf dropped the gun.

"Kick it behind ya."

He obliged. "What're ya doin'?"

"What're you doin'?"

"Target practice."

"On a live target?"

"Just a damn Yankee."

"He ain't done you no harm."

Califf glanced around. No Reuben.

"Friend's gone. Mustn't have cottoned to shootin' an unarmed man, Yankee'r no Yankee."

"Who're you? How you know he ain't armed?"

"Stop askin' questions an' git!"

"But I need my gun."

"Fetch it later. Go on, git!"

Although Califf's last shot had just missed Harriman's head, Harriman was oblivious to it or anything else except a path to the farmhouse. When he reached it, he paused, and walked around it, mesmerized. In the front of the yard, he saw something lying on the ground. When he came closer and saw what it was, his legs buckled. He collapsed and curled up in a ball, shivering, his head buried in his arms...

The deserters had shown no further desire to rush the house after the first few volleys. Instead, they sniped if they saw any movement in the windows and called out a continuing chorus of insults and taunts. With nightfall approaching, they were confident no Yankee relief would be coming.

The last rays of setting sun cast spider webs of golden light across the courtyard and illuminated several butternut corpses stiffening in death. One corpse in particular lay with his arms reaching to the sky, rigid fingers clutching air.

The men were quiet, weighing their chances, saying their prayers. The clock chimed again.

Harriman pulled the clock out of his saddlebag.

"Get down, will ya!" Alonzo ordered. A round shattered the window and embedded itself in the wall, as if it had heard his command. "Har, wait, don't!"

Harriman smashed the window and flung the clock out into the yard. "Here's a Christmas present for you, compliments of Colonel Walter Ridley!" The clock jangled as it hit the ground. Harriman fired a round into it. The clock hopped and spun crazily on the ground. Its face stared back at Harriman, springs protruding from a neat hole perforating it dead center. It read 4:44.

The deserters, unsure of what was happening, fired a flurry of shots at the sudden movement. Dust kicked up around the clock and more shots hit home, then all was silent again.

After a few moments, Alonzo said quietly, "Okay, boys. Time. We go two, one, two, cuz Wilkerson's dead. Remember, head east once you clear here. Ready, Har?"

Harriman nodded.

Alonzo went to the window and carefully selected a target for each man to shoot in their first volley. On Alonzo's cue, Harriman flung the door open. Bullets crashed into the door. The Yankees responded, shooting rapidly. Three deserters inching toward the house were killed instantly, as were two others hiding behind a water trough. The others ran for cover, recoiling at how fast and how many slugs were coming their way.

"Go!" Alonzo yelled and whacked the rump of McDowell's horse. Pent up in the cramped space, the horse flew out the door, with McDowell holding on for dear life. As he barreled out of the house, McDowell shot a deserter in the head at point blank range as the man charged onto the porch. Then he galloped for the woods.

Now it was Burleigh's turn. As he bolted out the shattered door, a volley blew him off his saddle. He was dead by the time he hit the floor, gaping holes in his chest. The riderless horse galloped into the falling darkness.

Crawford was about to leave when Alonzo called out for him to hold up. "Gotta reload." Alonzo checked and saw that Burleigh was dead. "Okay, Crawford. GO!"

Alonzo and Harriman lay down covering fire as Crawford reached the nearby woods and disappeared.

"Y'all set, Har?"

"You first," said Harriman. "You always are."

"I ain't never done this to you before, an' I won't do it again, but I'm pullin' rank." Alonzo slapped Harriman's chestnut across its rump and fired rapidly as Harriman's horse charged out the door.

"Damn you, Amos!" Harriman yelled, shooting from the hip as he rode past deserters dodging and scattering out of his way in the near darkness.

"Hate when you call me that!" Alonzo shouted.

Harriman rode low in the saddle, Indian-style, and collided with Cocked Hat, who seemed to have risen out of the ground. Harriman ran him over and sped away. When he reached the trees, Harriman turned around and fired as fast as he could to cover Alonzo's escape. He saw Alonzo riding hard behind him, also low in the saddle, the way Owen Hickenlooper had taught them.

Alonzo was almost to the woods when he lurched forward in the saddle and threw his arm around the horse's neck. Several more bullets hit the horse, breaking its stride and sending Alonzo sprawling to the ground.

Harriman rode back to his brother amid a hail of lead and lifted him over his saddle. Another bullet hit his horse in the neck. It whinnied and shied, but he managed to get to the nearby woods, leaving the leaderless, scattered deserters frantically gathering their horses to give chase. "Get your arms around me," Harriman said. "Hold on."

"S' bad, Har."

Navigating the low-lying branches and tree roots in the dark woods was difficult for the stricken horse. Its breathing was labored and bloody foam soon bubbled out of its mouth and nostrils. Each time the horse stumbled, Alonzo groaned. Several times he nearly fell off.

They stumbled around in the encroaching darkness for what seemed like an eternity. Harriman guided the horse with one hand and held onto Alonzo with the other, while constantly turning and listening for sounds of Rebel pursuit.

The horse finally collapsed. Harriman did his best to shield his brother from the fall. He lay Alonzo down in the darkness and listened for a long time. He heard the faint gurgling of running water. Groping in the darkness, he followed the sound to a small stream, where he filled his canteen.

As he returned to his brother, he fell into a large hole left by the torn-out roots of a toppled tree. The roots scratched his face and snarled his clothes as he clambered back to Alonzo. He dripped water into Alonzo's mouth. The sounds of men and horses echoed far off in the woods. Harriman gingerly felt around Alonzo's back and found an entry hole close to the spine.

"Can't feel my feet," Alonzo whispered. He sighed and closed his eyes. "I'm done. Leave me."

"I'm not leaving you."

"I'll miss walkin' together in the victory parade."

Oncoming voices called out. Torches threw off eerie shadows in the forest undergrowth. The deserters were methodical, encircling an area, then closing it down.

Harriman managed to gently navigate Alonzo into the uprooted tree hole. He dropped into the hole beside him, pulled some more leaves and branches over them both, and held his shivering brother in his arms.

Waiting.

Listening to the deserters' voices echoing in the forest, their torches playing shadow dances in the trees, he drifted sleepily back, carried along on the familiar smell of his brother's body, to a lifetime of nights spent together, sleeping under the stars. He was startled by insects crawling for the moist warmth under his pants and shirt.

"Here, boys. A Yank lost his ride." There were cackles and hoots in the distance. "Can't a gotten far on foot. Never git back to his lines tonight. It's as black as Sherman's heart out here."

"Let's get 'em in the mornin'." Other voices agreed.

The deserters faded off into the darkness. The crickets and the running stream returned to their song in the now quiet woods.

"Can't feel my legs," Alonzo croaked.

Harriman flagged under a sudden wave of exhaustion. He would figure out how to get them back in the morning. Tomorrow was an infinity away. Right now, it was warm down in the hole with his brother, and he did everything he could to make Alonzo as comfortable as possible. Harriman was so tired. He needed to sleep, just for a little while. The morning would make everything right, just like it always had, each and every day, come what may.

Alonzo quivered and sighed. Harriman pulled him closer. When sleep did come, and it came mercifully fast, he dreamed he was back in Iowa, running through a cornfield, chasing his brother into a golden sunlit wheatfield. Once, he felt Alonzo stir and he pulled him closer, then fell back to sleep.

The birds woke him at first light. Harriman stirred in the hole. For a moment, he did not know where he was. A mouthful of dirt and the weight leaning on him brought him to his senses. He pushed the weight off him and gagged when he saw Alonzo staring at him through sightless eyes, inches from his face.

Leaves rustled nearby. He held his breath. The rustling sounds drew closer. Harriman felt for his pistol and drew it, ready to make his last stand. He saw a soldier sitting astride a horse, letting the horse graze, the reins hanging from its neck. Harriman aimed the pistol.

"McDowell?" Harriman whispered.

McDowell lifted his head. The trooper's face was raked by long gashes, dried blood caked to his cheeks. "Hickenlooper, is that you?"

"What happened to you? I thought you made it out."

"It got too dark to ride so I hid out in a barn until daybreak. You know where we are? Where're the others?"

Harriman dropped to his knees and scratched at the ground with his hands.

"What the hell you doin'?" McDowell asked.

Harriman struggled to lift Alonzo's rigid corpse out of the hole.

"I'm sorry, Hickenlooper." He dismounted and helped Harriman with Alonzo's body.

Off in the distance, the baying of searching hounds froze them. After a beat, Harriman scratched even more furiously, but still could not make any headway against the hard ground. He took the butt end of his Colt and pawed the earth, grunting and cursing. He scratched and clawed at the ground until his fingers were bloody and raw, tears flowing down his cheeks as he dug.

The dogs bayed closer and more urgently now, indicating they had picked up a scent.

"C'mon, Hickenlooper. Nothin' more can be done for him. We gotta go."

Birds scattered overhead. The horse's nostrils flared, smelling danger.

McDowell mounted his horse, checked his rifle and twisted in the saddle. "Goddamn it! I'm sorry about your brother, but I ain't dyin' for no dead man."

Harriman choked back sobs as he covered his brother with branches and leaves as best he could.

"If it means anything to ya, Alonzo don't care a whiff what happens to him. I'm sure he'd want ya to save yerself," McDowell said in a gentle whisper.

Harriman sobbed into the saddlebags and grasped McDowell's offered hand. Finally, he pulled himself up on the horse.

They rode most of that morning. McDowell kept to the reverse path of the sun while staying in the forests to keep out of sight. Harriman stared blankly ahead and rebuffed McDowell's few attempts at conversation. Several times, they hid out to avoid Rebel cavalry. Occasionally, McDowell stopped when he felt Harriman's sobs well up and just let the color bearer weep.

"S'okay. He's in a better place than we are."

The going got harder when it started to rain. They had to slow their pace. They rested and watered the horse more frequently to let it rest from carrying twice its normal load. The country seemed to sprout more Rebel cavalry patrols, so they felt they must be close to the Union column.

The tensest moment came when they reached Army of the Tennessee pickets at nightfall. Pickets were seriously on edge this deep in Rebel country, and any mistake identifying oneself could be the last. A sentry fired at them because they didn't know that day's password.

Harriman was summoned to Colonel Ridley's tent when he got back.

"I understand you ran into some trouble."

"We lost three men, one missing, probably dead, five horses and all the forage."

"Who didn't make it?"

"Crawford, Wilkerson and my brother are dead. Burleigh's missing." *Harriman drew in a deep breath as grief washed over him again.*

"A shame."

"Don't say that."

"Excuse me?"

"It was Chattanooga."

"You're upset, Corporal."

"That look in your eye when we got to the top of Mission Ridge. It must have killed you you couldn't press charges against us for disobeying orders, the way it turned out.

You've had it in for us ever since. Sending us on this goddamn patrol was your revenge."

"How dare you."

"How dare you! Come to think of it, you've had it in for us ever since we voted for Damon Granger to lead this regiment."

"That is patently absu..."

Harriman held up his hand.

"Are you threatening me?" Ridley jumped to his feet. "I'll have you shot."

"I'm not threatening you. I'm telling you. Somehow, someday, I will square our accounts. You won't shoot me."

"No?"

"No. It wouldn't look so good you sent out an under-strength patrol and got three men killed for a goddamn clock, then shot one of the survivors."

"How are you going to prove that?"

"It's my word against yours. I'm a corporal, you're a colonel. I'm not gonna say anything. But my brother's dead on account of you."

An orderly peered into the tent. "Everything okay, sir?"

Ridley and Harriman locked eyes. Ridley waved the orderly away.

Harriman rose to go, then paused by the tent flap. "What time is it?"

"What?"

"I shot it."

"Shot what?"

"Your goddamn clock."

Ridley scowled and shook his head. Then he brightened. "Not only is it your word against mine, but there's no clock you claim I asked you to get. I am sorry about your brother, Hickenlooper. Truly I am. We will forget about this. Dismissed."

CHAPTER 36

Harriman stirred on the ground. Although it was colder in the late afternoon, beads of sweat dripped off his brow. He opened his eyes and fixed on what he had seen before he passed out. It was a clock, a bullet hole through the center of its face. It still read 4:44. He reached for the clock and put it in his sack. Parts of it fell onto the ground, but he left them.

He returned to the house. Sections of the roof had fallen in. Bullet holes pocked the doorframe and windows. He walked into the large main room. Looters had long since made off with everything except for the skeletons of a horse and the dead trooper Wilkerson lying beneath it. They had stripped what clothing they could off the corpse. A few brass bullet jackets littered the floor. Seeing the room again, it surprised him how they could have packed themselves into that space.

There was a slight rustling.

Harriman swiveled to a clump of nearby bushes and undergrowth. It reinforced his feeling that he was being watched constantly from a distance, but whatever presence there was never made itself known. Maybe it was the ghosts of his journey.

Which was the east window? He looked up to check where the sun was now. The sky was a steel gray overcast. He walked into the woods, recalling that Alonzo's horse had gone down as it had made it to the trees. Sure enough, there was another horse's skeleton, picked clean of its flesh, its saddle and blanket roll gone. He guessed the horse that had carried Alonzo and him away from the battle had walked maybe a half-hour before it died. He remembered they had followed a rough farm track. He found it soon enough, and followed it until he recognized what he was looking for.

Skeletal tree roots reached up from the forest floor. As if there was someone trying to beat him to his discovery, he sprinted toward the uprooted tree. As he neared it, he realized he was humming "Marching Through Georgia" again, and choked. He dropped to his knees by the large hole and pawed at the branches and earth until he felt something hard. His humming and digging stopped. Sitting back on his haunches, he took several deep breaths, then commenced digging. He found the tattered remains of a blue forage cap with a faded gold "D" stamped onto the rotted crown. Taking another deep breath, he delved deeper into the hole.

Maggots and rodents had left only bones, making his work easier, because he could grab onto bone without his hands slipping on rotten flesh. He was methodical in his work. He saw an image of Lucinda carefully tending to her mother. He handled Alonzo's remains with a fanatical attention to cleaning and stacking everything he uncovered. A wave of self-loathing washed over him and he retched. He sat next to the pile of cleaned bones, staring into the forest and the past.

The shrieks of birds roused him. They're stealing Alonzo! They're laughing at me! He instinctively reached for the bones and relaxed when he saw them lying next to him. He remembered an innocent promise he made to his brother a lifetime ago. It was the one he had not kept. As he put each bone in his sack, he found it harder to breathe. Gasping, his pain burst open, in wails, then in animal shrieks, each one ripping deeper into the hushed forest and gouging out his insides. Any living things in that forest became still, listening to the blue two-legged beast howling and clutching a bag of bones.

After a while, his crying softened and his breathing steadied. He was crying now because he hated being alive.

CHAPTER 37

Lucinda and Rufus had followed Harriman from what she thought was a safe distance, but one time he had suddenly looked up, forcing them deeper into cover. Rufus had wanted to go to him, especially to help him bury the bones. But Lucinda knew it was best to leave him alone.

She had remained motionless, listening to the growing crescendo of his sobs and wails. She held her breath for so long, she got dizzy and gasped for air. His overpowering grief triggered her own, and she shoved her fist into her mouth to hold back her sobs so he would not know she was there.

Rufus was so aghast at the sight and sounds he witnessed that when he tried to write in his diary, he had to cover his ears. Finally he slipped away.

A hunger and thirst clawed at Lucinda. Her mouth was parched. But watching him there, she now felt a deep desire to show herself to him, to let him see she was bearing witness to his loss, like he had done before with her. She moved out of hiding and sat down across from him, carefully tucking in a bone protruding from the sack by his side. She watched his body quiver in arrhythmic spasms.

Harriman sensed her and looked up. His hair was matted with chunks of red earth. Tears had left dirty tracks on his cheeks. His reddened eyes stared through hers to someplace far away. When they fixed on her, they held a look she had never seen on a human being before. A fear grabbed her that he had departed this world and no longer knew who she was.

"Who's that?" she asked, pointing at the sack.

"Leave me alone."

"Someone you knew."

"Leave…"

"Ain't goin nowhere, so don't say it agin. Who is it?"

"My brother."

Lucinda saw the rotten blue forage cap lying by his side. "We followed you. Saw everything."

"I told you to wait for me."

"You think you killed Ford, right?"

He nodded. "Don't you?"

Lucinda reached into the folds of her dress and unfurled a cloth. "Ya don' know how much I hated you when you showed up at my door. Ya dared come to my house, makin' like you knew Ford, when all along you was his killer. Ya didn't fool me. After we buried Momma I remembered ya told me yer dream, the one yer always havin'." She handed him something. "I found this where Ford died."

He stared at what was in his hand and couldn't make sense of it. He looked closer. It was two bullets, perfectly fused together. "Like in my dream."

Lucinda nodded. "Never know fer certain ya killed Ford. I suspect you did, but you were followin' the rules, kill or be killed. What I know ya did is brought Ford home to my Momma. One thing I'm sure of, this world's cryin' out fer people who make things better than they were." She let out a cackle.

"What's so funny?"

"Ya got her riled up."

"Who?"

"Momma. She was so peeved ya woke her up with all yer wailin'! Ya know what she said to me the other night? She came to me when I had a knife to yer throat. She said, 'Daughter, any man comes this far to make things right is a man deserves fergivin'." She took his hand in hers and squeezed it shut around the fused bullets. "Keep 'em. Maybe they'll let ya sleep better." She stroked his face and pushed some loose strands of hair away.

Tears rolled down his cheeks as he bent to her touch. He broke down again.

Lucinda laid his head in her lap and stroked his hair, pulling out pieces of earth. She rocked him gently and hummed the lullaby her momma used to sing to her. Her tears fell in his dirty blond hair, on the blue forage cap, into the red clay earth, and she smiled down at the man now sleeping tenderly in her arms.

Lucinda awoke to the sounds of digging. She was lying under his blue overcoat. She saw Harriman watching her, smiling the most beautiful smile she had ever seen, glad he still could. She stretched her body out full length, letting the coat fall off her. She pulled it back over her and reached her arms to the sky. Her toes dug into the red earth and she let out a screech, startling the birds, who answered with screeches of their own as they flitted through the trees.

"Good morning to you, too," Harriman said. "I'd offer you some coffee, but I don't have any."

"Don' touch the stuff—makes me twitchy," she teased. "I fly around pretty good as it is. How long ya been lookin' at me?"

"I've been looking for you my whole life." Harriman leaned over and kissed her. She met his lips tenderly. They looked at each with wonder and affection.

They had slept on a knoll overlooking a glen, now covered in rays of morning sunlight. Near where she lay, he had found a spot soft enough to dig a grave, which he and Rufus had finished.

Harriman carved an epitaph on a cross he'd made of boards scavenged from the farmhouse. He placed Alonzo's bones in the hole and began to cover it up. Something stopped him and he reached down into the grave. He pulled out Alonzo's rotted forage cap.

"What're you doin?" Rufus asked.

"Let 'em keep the hat," Lucinda said.

"I agree." A figure emerged from the bushes. It was Jed.

"So it's you who's been following us, watching us," Rufus said.

"Who's he?" Lucinda asked.

"Sea Island sounds good, eh?" Rufus asked.

Jed nodded. "The lady's right, suh. Let yo' brother keep the hat."

Harriman pulled off the little gold "Co. D" from the forage cap and placed it back in the grave. They stood in silence as he filled the hole and tapped the cross into the earth. This is what he carved on it:

AMOS ALONZO HICKENLOOPER

6TH VOL. IOWA INF.

JULY 23, 1842 – DEC. 7, 1864

NEVER FORGOTTEN

Harriman knelt down opposite the cross and clasped his hands together. "I kept my word, Amos. I hope you know that."

Lucinda squeezed his shoulder. "Course he knows. An' even if he don't, we do."

CHAPTER 38

A tired and grumpy Jack Connolly trudged home. As the days got closer to Christmas and New Year's, people were continuously asking him about the progress of the color bearer.

"What news?"

He didn't have any.

"Think he'll make it?"

His pat answer, "I wouldn't bet on it," usually got more of a wince than a smile.

He admitted it: he'd lagged behind the story from the beginning. The kid had scooped him. What would it have cost to hire the kid like he had requested? And why didn't he see the story like the kid had? It was a firsthand scoop on a one-man peace march, for Christ's sake. With the furor in Washington, moves to impeach President Johnson developing momentum, and everyone arguing whether the South should be part of the United States, he had missed it.

Connolly entered his darkened house. His housekeeper, Mrs. O'Reilly, greeted him and took his hat and coat.

"How is she?"

"She's resting fine, Mr. Connolly. Doctor Simpson was by earlier and gave her something to help her sleep. Would you care for something? I fixed some potatoes and gravy for you."

"Not much of an appetite, Mrs. O'Reilly. No need for you to stay."

"You sure? I don't mind, sir."

"No, you go on home. Thank you."

Connolly climbed the stairs, past the pictures, framed headlines and assorted hitching posts in the life he'd shared with the woman dying upstairs.

Turning at the top, he peered into the room she'd kept the way it was the day their Jonah left for the war, never to return. He felt the world inside this house getting smaller and tugging at him with the tiniest details he'd never bothered about before—their bedroom door that did not close shut, so they'd always had to be extra quiet when they made love; the creaking eighth stair from the landing, the one that always gave Jonah away whenever he'd try to slip home later than he'd been told to; the peculiar sighs the house emanated on winter nights when the wind blew in from the north against their bedroom wall.

He entered the bedroom softly, not that Victoria could hear him, but he did it out of the habit of coming home late and wanting to let her sleep. She never did. Those nights he had deadlines, she would wait until he'd undressed, letting him think that he'd successfully slipped in, then out of the darkness ask him about his day.

She wasn't asking now. He stared at the frail, withered woman making cooing sounds in her drug-induced sleep. Suddenly she winced and moaned as a shot of cancerous pain coursed through her. It surged through him, too, and he winced and caught his breath before sitting down next to her, taking her hand in his.

"Being as how it's late in the day, there are some things I have to say. V, I'm a proud man, you've always known that, and I don't admit when I'm wrong nearly enough. But I've been wrong not to be sure I let you know each and every day what you mean to me. Every day I didn't tell you how much I appreciate that you've given me a life to follow my dream, I've been wrong. How you've carried my grief for our boy on top of your own, as if it were all your own, so I could bury myself in my work, I've been wrong. The times I criticized you for buying the few things that made you happy, knowing that you were making do without many more things your friends have so I could make this paper the best it could be, I was wrong. And now, I have missed this story. I'm wrong about that, too." His words trailed off.

Suddenly he felt a pulse shoot through his hand. She had heard him, from somewhere. And in that short little squeeze she sent him, she let him know it was going to be okay.

CHAPTER 39

The trees pushed in on both sides of the narrow lane. A nasal voice called out: "Stop right there, Yank, an' let the girl go."

"He means no harm," Lucinda answered.

"Ya come down here, stirring up trouble with this march, this damn bet ya made. We seen enough trouble, goddamnit! Let her go." There was the unmistakable sound of a musket being cocked.

"You best go," Harriman whispered.

Lucinda took his arm in hers. "C'mon out and show yer face, ya damn coward. Shoot an unarmed man. Ya should be ashamed a' yerself." They kept walking slowly down the road. A shot rang out, the bullet kicking up dust between Rufus and Jed.

"Ain't gonna warn ya again."

"Go, before you get hurt," Harriman implored Lucinda.

"No."

"Damn ya!" screamed the voice. "If I don' do it, don't ya know sumbody else will!" But no other shots came. "Yer crazy, Yank. You too, missy!"

"I think he's right," Rufus muttered. He was walking awkwardly, like he had something stuck between his legs.

"You okay?" Lucinda asked. She glanced down and noticed a dark stain spreading on his pants. She cackled.

Rufus flushed crimson. "It's not funny!"

"Well, I'll be. You've seen the elephant," Harriman said.

They reached a small, nondescript hamlet consisting of a few houses, a blacksmith shop, a small church and a graveyard. What was noteworthy was a detachment of federal cavalry milling around in the center of the settlement.

They went to the small church and looked in when they heard the sound of children echoing a single woman's voice.

Rufus approached two soldiers standing in the doorway. "Mind if I ask what's going on?"

"See for yourself," a surly young trooper gestured, eyeing Lucinda.

It was a spare country church with but a few wooden pews, a small simple altar, an upright piano and a cross hanging on the wall behind the pulpit. A group of black children ranging in ages from seven to fifteen sat in the pews, facing an elderly white woman dressed in black, holding a long pointing stick which she tapped rhythmically on a chalkboard at the front of the altar. The woman recited the alphabet. The children followed along haltingly. Jed sat down in the back pew, fascinated. One of the older boys spied the travelers watching from the back of the room. He elbowed his neighbor. The children fell silent.

"Children, eyes and ears here, please." The woman rapped the board with her stick and continued in a brisk, serious manner, casting a frustrated look at the newcomers. The children worked their way to the end of the alphabet. Several blacks, obviously their parents, watched from the back of the room.

The prim woman folded up her pointer. "Very good, children. That's all for today." She spoke to their parents in the back of the room. "I will be back here at this time in two weeks. Be prompt, please. Class dismissed." The children sat still, not understanding. The woman brushed the air with her hands. "Class is over. Run along now."

The children bounded out of the church with their parents trailing behind. The woman collected her books and folded the chalkboard under her arm. "Can I help you?"

"Uh, no. I was just wondering what you were doing here, if you don't mind me asking," Harriman said.

"I am teaching the local children to read. Was it that unclear?" She managed a wry smile.

"You ain't from here," Lucinda said.

"How can you tell? No, I work for the Christian Commission. Boston, Massachusetts chapter. My name is Willa Henry." She extended a hand to Lucinda.

"A long way to come teach nigger children," Lucinda said, not taking it.

Willa Henry bridled. "I don't just teach Negro children. I encourage all the children to attend. White families haven't chosen to do so, yet."

"Why's the niggers so special?" Lucinda asked.

Jed slipped out the door.

"They're not. They have a lot of catching up to do."

"I never had no schoolin'," Lucinda said and walked out.

"She's like those kids. She can't read, either." Harriman shrugged. "I admire what you're doing."

"It's the least I can do as a Christian, given the situation I have found here. Are you with the occupation forces?" Willa asked.

"No."

"Why are you here then?"

"It's a long story, but it's the least I can do as a Christian."

Willa nodded. "We must all do our part to put this terrible war behind us." She pulled a man's watch and fob from her purse. "Oh, dear." She drew him in a little closer. "I must go. I have a class in Averasboro. I can see that my escorts are none too pleased to accompany me, so that when I don't keep to my schedule, they get even more cross. God speed for whatever His plan is for you."

Harriman shook her hand. "God speed."

Outside the church one of the soldiers was trying to chat up Lucinda, who ignored him. The soldier backed away when Harriman and Willa came out.

"Gentlemen, let's be off. We can't be late, now can we?" She offered up her hand. Harriman assisted her onto the wagon.

"Shit detail," the soldier mumbled under his breath.

Harriman turned on him. "You ought to be grateful. There are far worse."

"Oh, yeah. What do you know about it?" the trooper spat back.

"Come, come," Willa called from the coach. It pulled out of the hamlet as a procession of wagons met at the crossroads.

Diary entry of December 19th, 1867:

I witnessed some ex-slave and white families meet at a small country crossroads. Their wagons were stacked high with everything they could carry—furniture, trunks, dishes, clothes. The wagons leaned precariously under their weights. What would happen if a wagon wheel broke or a horse buckled under the strain? It would be a disaster.

The horses moved slowly, pulling a pile of possessions too large for the wagons, but so small for a lifetime. As they passed each other, no one said a word, but in that moment I saw them experience common bonds of homelessness and despair.

I heard Jed say, "Mebbe dem white folks knows how it feels now, walkin' in our shoes."

CHAPTER 40

Harriman heard the rushing water long before they reached the Ogeechee. The river was running high and fast. A bloated baby doe floated by, caught in a large tree branch, sightless eyes staring into the gray sky. Scanning the far bank, Hickenlooper shivered as he splashed the cold water on his face and drank a few mouthfuls.

"S'wrong?" Lucinda asked.

"We can't cross here."

"Probly nowhere until the water drops. Be a day or two if it don't rain s'more."

Rufus and Jed went off to gather wood. Harriman made a circle of rocks for a firepit. Lucinda wandered off. When a shot rang out, Harriman tore off after her, but a few minutes later they emerged together with a dead cottontail. Lucinda dropped it on a large stone and commenced to skin it. Before long, the smell of roasting rabbit had them all eager for dinner.

"What will you do when we get to Savannah?" Rufus asked Lucinda.

"Find work. Savannah's big, I heard. Poppa was there once. Said the houses were pretty as could be, but everyone rushed around too much. I'll take it a day at a time."

"I still don't understand why you burned down your house?" Rufus asked. "Can you explain that?"

"Nuthin there but ghosts. Couldn't stand the idea of strangers movin' in, livin' there scot free, after all we done to make it our own. No." She shook her head vehemently. "An' I wanted to see how yer bet turned out."

"Rufus, what day is it?"

"December 21st. It's getting tight, Mr. Hickenlooper," Rufus replied.

"You still think I'll win it?"

"Y'already have," Lucinda said.

"How's that?" Harriman asked.

"Being true to Ford, to yer brother, most of all, true to your word, ya won more'n any bet. So serious." She touched his cheek and kissed him, tentatively at first, then long and deep.

"Come back with me," Harriman whispered in her ear. He tensed when he spotted something behind her.

"What?" She turned.

A lone rider had emerged from the woods on the opposite side of the river several hundred yards away. The rider had relaxed the reins to let his mount drink and was looking around in all directions. He sniffed the wind, examined the ground, then pulled off a red bandanna from around his forehead and wiped his brow.

"Let's go," Harriman said, grabbing his walking stick and pack. "C'mon, everyone. Gather your things quickly. Leave the fire."

"Who is it?"

"I don't know, and I don't want to find out."

He crouched down and moved swiftly into the underbrush with Lucinda, Rufus and Jed in tow. They kept moving for a long time. As the sky darkened, they came to a bend in the river that afforded them good sight lines up and downstream. Here the river narrowed, offering a better chance of crossing the next day. They found a carved-out section of riverbank under which they settled for the night.

Harriman cursed himself for allowing Lucinda to come along, while at the same time cherished the warmth of her body nestled against him in the darkness. They lay in silence, lost in thought, and finally drifted into a restless sleep.

Sometime in the middle of the night, an explosion jarred Harriman awake. The thunder rolled away across the sky. Water dripped onto his head. Another thunderclap sounded, this time closer. Lightning lit up the river. It had started raining again. The river was running high and fast. He looked over and was surprised to see Lucinda sitting up, watching the river too, her knees tucked up against her chest.

"What?" Harriman asked.

"Thinkin' bout those kids we found."

Harriman stared into the water and sighed. "I've thought about them, too." He held out his hand. "How old are you?"

"Why? Sixteen."

"You could have been one of those kids."

She took his hand. "I'm not."

"Go back to sleep," he said, stroking her hair.

She smiled and curled up next to him. "Unh-unh."

"Me, neither."

They watched the patterns of the rain play on the water and finally fell asleep to the sound of the river gurgling by.

By the next morning the rain had stopped. Droplets fell from the rim of the embankment onto them. Harriman sat up stiffly and stretched, covering Lucinda with the blanket they shared.

He walked to the river's edge and splashed water on his face, examining the current moving swiftly past him. The river had risen again. He wiped his face off and saw the same man he'd seen the day before watching him from the same side of the river about a hundred yards upstream.

The man spurred his horse and slowly approached their campsite.

Harriman went to Lucinda and nudged her. She stirred and moaned. He nudged her harder.

"Ow! Mornin' to you, too," she groaned.

"Act like nothing's wrong and move away from me. Slowly."

Lucinda peered around Harriman, saw the rider and recognized him. Red Hundley!

She dug out her Colt.

Harriman shoved it back out of sight. "Put it away. Whatever happens, no guns."

Red pulled his horse up within yards of them, his hands resting on the pommel of his saddle. "Mornin'."

"Morning," Harriman answered.

"I was speakin' to Miss McWhorter. Y'all right, Lucinda?"

"I'm fine, Red."

"You know each other?" Harriman asked.

"Known him a long time. He's a neighbor."

"Was a neighbor. Yankees burned yer place down, Lucinda. Saw 'em do it."

Harriman, Lucinda and Rufus exchanged puzzled looks. Before Lucinda could explain, Red moved his horse in closer.

"Say, I was wondrin' if any a you seen someone. I'm lookin' fer an old nigger, foreman at the Ball place over near Macon. Seems he was stolen."

Red dismounted and walked over to the group. Rufus gave him a wide berth. Red noticed Harriman's walking stick.

"Ya mind?" Without getting a reply, he picked up the stick and examined the flag. "Hunh. Who're you?"

"Name's Hickenlooper."

"Where're ya from?"

"Iowa."

Red clucked softly, smiled and drew his pistol. Harriman stepped in front of Lucinda, seeing she was reaching for the Colt. From behind his back, he grabbed her hand and held it.

"Seems this nigger disappeared when a Yank and a young kid, kinda like you two as a matter of fact, paid a visit to Mr. Ball. Mr. Ball wants him back." Red trained the Colt on Harriman. "Okay, Iowa, whaddya say?"

"We didn't steal anybody."

Red cracked the pistol across Harriman's face, opening a gash over his eye. "Did I say you did? You're real quick to deny it."

Out of the corner of his eye, Harriman saw Lucinda's Colt coming up.

"NO!"

Red grabbed Harriman and held the gun to his head. "Drop the shooter, Miss McWhorter, or Chickencoop here is gonna get real dead." Red spoke in a sing-song voice, as though he was talking to an infant. "Do it."

Lucinda dropped the Colt.

"That's better. Now, where's the nigger?"

"Here, suh."

Red turned and caught a six inch-thick oak branch across his forehead. He dropped to the ground.

Lucinda scooped up his pistol.

"For an old man, you sure got some heft left," Rufus said.

Jed smiled as he stepped over Red. "Sea Island calling mighty loud right now. Ain't never hit no white man."

"How you fit in all this?" Lucinda asked.

"I'm the nigger what ain't been stolen, Miss Lucinda."

"Why'd Ball tell him you were stolen?" Rufus asked.

"Masta Ball musta been plenty mad I left. Hired hisself a bounty man. Can't have no one uppin' and leavin'. Bad example t'others."

"Bounty hunters catch escaped criminals. You claimed your freedom," Harriman said.

Red rose shakily to his feet, clutching his head, eyes livid.

"You're mistaken, mister. I suggest you walk away," Harriman said.

"This nigger's goin' back to his rightful owner."

"This man is going where he wants to go. You try to stop him, you have to get through me first."

Lucinda stepped between them. "Enough! Leave it be, Red. This Ball feller lied to you. You kin see there's been a mistake."

"Only mistake was not shootin' Iowa when I could of."

"He's not listening," Harriman said. "Step away, Lucinda."

Rufus took Lucinda by the arm, but she pulled away. She kept her Colt trained on Red as she moved back.

Harriman and Red circled each other. Blood trickled into Harriman's eye from the pistol cut. He wiped at it just as Red rushed him. Harriman stepped aside and threw Red to the ground.

Red came up in a flash. They circled again. Red closed the distance and landed a punch to the jaw. Red grabbed a rock and lunged at Harriman.

Harriman grabbed Red's wrist and twisted as he fell away from the blow, nearly breaking it as he pulled it across his knee, forcing the rock free. He came up and wrapped his arms under Red's armpits in a bear hug. The two men's faces were inches apart.

Red kicked and tugged, flailing his arms and legs, trying to knee Harriman in the groin.

Harriman was in too close for the blows to generate any power. He lifted Red off the ground and drove him against his knee without letting go of him. The two men lurched and swayed over the rocky shoreline, as if in a drunken embrace, grunting and swearing.

As Harriman squeezed harder, Red's face began to turn red. His attempts to break free weakened. Spittle bubbled out of his mouth and his eyes rolled back up in his head. He hurled a wad of spit in Harriman's eyes and tried to bite his ear. Harriman stared into his eyes and squeezed harder. There were two loud pops, the sounds of ribs cracking.

Red screamed and collapsed to the ground, rolling and clutching his chest.

Harriman removed the cavalry carbine from Red's saddle holster, and tossed it to Rufus. He led the horse over to Red. "No one stole him. Jed left of his own free will. Got that? Now get up and move out."

Red struggled onto the horse and said nothing.

"Suit yourself. Ball knows the truth, even if you don't see it. Take it up with him." Harriman slapped the horse's butt. It took off with Red holding onto the reins, bent over the saddle. Harriman spotted

Red's bandanna lying on the ground and dipped it in the water, swabbing his bleeding cut. "So he's your neighbor? Small world."

Lucinda grabbed the bandanna and cleaned the gash.

"His family lived a few miles away. We'd get together fer holidays sometimes. I'd see him at town meetins. He was sorta close to my older brother Holcomb."

"Did he fancy you?"

"He's way too old."

"Then so am I," he smiled.

Lucinda blushed.

"We better move now. I want to put distance between us and that neighbor of yours. We need to find a good place to cross." Harriman gathered his things.

"Harriman can't cross that river. He can't cross any river," Rufus whispered to Lucinda.

"How come?"

"He can't swim."

"An' I can't read. An' you can't hold your water when someone's shootin' at ya. So what? We'll do it." She pocketed the Colt and followed Harriman down the shoreline with Jed and Rufus in tow.

The skies rumbled and lightning crisscrossed the darkening sky when they stopped at the river's edge. They made camp.

Harriman watched the river. A shiver ran through him.

"What?" Lucinda asked.

"Just a chill."

Jed sat on a log off by himself. "Why didn't you run away with Sherman's troops?" Jed looked up, surprised Rufus was making conversation.

"I did."

"I don't understand."

Jed kicked the stones at his feet "Me' n Juno, Juno my wife, an' our girl Violet, we left Culloden and followed Sherman's army. Lots of folks doin' the same thing, leavin' to hitch onto the Yankees.

Saw people I hadn't seen since I got sold to Massa Ball's poppa way back when. Like a rollin' reunion on the road. We was singin' songs, dancin and laughin'. It truly was the day'a Jubilo." He smiled that grimacing smile at the memory.

"We get to this here river, the Ogeechee. River's flooded. I'm wondrin' how we gonna git across. De Yankees, they made a bridge, jes' like it was nuthin'. Tied ropes to boats, stretched 'em across, laid planks over de boats, and walked over, horses, wagons, guns. When they git across, some of us follow. Watchin' that river movin so angry, I git scared, tell Juno an' Violet to stay put, wait 'til the river settle down. Someone shout, 'Rebbie cavary!' Folks start pushin' to get across the bridge. Before I knows it, Juno an' Violet goin' across, too. I'se tryin' to tell em de river take 'em to hell. But Juno, all she say, 'any place better'n d here'."

"What happened?" Rufus asked, writing in his diary. "Did they make it across?"

Jed's shoulders quivered. He didn't answer.

"We cut the ropes," Harriman said.

CHAPTER 41

"By the time we reached the river, we were wet, exhausted and angry. The officers had been riding us hard that day because we hadn't made our fifteen miles yet and it was getting dark. Wheeler's cavalry had been harassing our rear for days. The water was high and moving fast. They called up the pontoniers. It was a wonder to see our engineers build roads and bridges, always under pressure, often under fire. I'm sure they gave the Rebels fits because they got us through swamps, across rivers, over mountains, it didn't matter what the terrain was. We kept moving." Harriman glanced at Jed, who was watching him through tearing eyes.

"When the pontoniers finished, everything moved across. Regiment after regiment crossed the high water. All day and night. By the next morning, everyone was across. The Sixth was one of the last, and when we crossed, we were ordered to cover the rear.

"The slaves watched and waited patiently for their turn. Once the last of our soldiers were across, the slaves started over. It wasn't long before that bridge was jammed with men, women and children holding onto the ropes while trying to keep their balance on the swaying bridge.

"Wheelers' cavalry caught up with us and started shooting and sabering the slaves who had not made it onto the bridge yet. The slaves on the bridge panicked and tried to run across, making the bridge sway more violently. People started falling in."

Rufus was scribbling feverishly.

"Put that away and just listen."

Rufus shoved the diary back in his pocket.

"Then Ridley ordered us to cut the ropes. I couldn't believe it," Harriman continued in a low, resigned voice. "I asked the colonel to reconsider. He insisted the slaves, 'stragglers', he called them, were slowing down the column. Besides, he said, we had to destroy the bridge so the Rebs couldn't use it.

"'They haven't been slowing us up. They've been right behind us the whole time,' I argued.

"'These orders come from the division commander. Cut the goddamn ropes or I'll have you arrested.'

"Slaves closest to our side of the river saw our troops cutting the ropes and tried to cross faster. The ones in the middle of the bridge turned back. Everyone was trying to escape in both directions. Some must have given up and jumped in the river. When the ropes got cut, everyone fell in the water.

"The Rebel cavalry sabered and shot all the slaves on their side of the river. They started picking off anyone they could see in the raging current and chasing after anybody who had escaped into the nearby woods. Me and some of the other Sixth boys tried to lay down fire to drive off the cavalry, but we started hitting slaves, so we gave up. I said to Ridley, 'The stragglers won't be holding us up anymore, sir.' He didn't answer and rode off."

Jed had moved away from the campsite down the river.

Harriman walked after him. "I'm sorry."

"Me, too, suh."

Harriman nodded.

"It ain't what ya think." Jed shook his head.

"What, then?"

"Ain't a day goes by, I wish I'da gone in dat river wid 'em."

He swiped at his eyes and coughed. "I's followin' ya since ya left Culloden."

"Why?"

"I been askin' myself de same ting. Why am I followin' de one got my family killed? De answer is, I seen what you doin' on this march a' yers. Truth is, I's moved to."

Harriman smiled. "I thought I saw you a few times. I felt something, a presence, always watching us, and when I looked, I'd see a branch moving or hear footsteps retreating into the forest."

"It's de wind."

"Can I quote you?" Rufus had joined them.

"Do what now?"

"Use the very same words you just said, about you and the wind, I mean. Can I quote you?"

"Ya kin quote me."

The next morning they arose before dawn. The river had fallen, so they prepared to cross. Harriman made a loop in a rope he had brought, and tried several times to hook it around a branch stump on a fallen log on the opposite bank, to no avail.

"I'll go first," Rufus suggested. "I'll secure the rope and you can hold onto it while you cross."

Harriman nodded. "Be careful." He wrapped one end of the rope around a tree stump, tied it off, and wrapped the other end of the rope around Rufus' waist.

Rufus waded into the river. The water was colder and faster than he anticipated. He used each step to gauge the depth and smoothness of the bottom. The bottom suddenly wasn't there, and he disappeared under the water. "I slipped. It's okay," he called out when he bobbed to the surface. The water was over his head in the middle of the river and the current was pulling him downstream, but he managed to swim across and touch bottom with his feet. He tied the rope to the branch stump and held it fast, then motioned for the others to come over.

"You're next, Jed," Harriman said. "You're not going to be watching us get across this time."

Jed took the rope and followed Rufus' route across the river as closely as he could.

"Now you."

"You first," Lucinda answered.

"Where I'm from, ladies go first. I'll be right behind you."

"You can't swim. I'll be behind you."

"I can hold a rope. Go."

Lucinda stepped into the water and pulled herself across easily. When she emerged from the water, her dress clung to her. She looked back at Harriman and caught him staring at her body pressed against her dress. She beckoned him over.

Harriman entered the water slowly. As the water rose to his shoulders, he felt the panic rising in him. He began to hum "Marching Through Georgia." The water got even deeper in the center of the river. Harriman could no longer touch bottom. He paused, tugged on the rope and continued to pull himself across. A sunken log he did not see caught him square in his side. He screamed and let go of the rope. He was immediately swept down river by the strong current. He flailed, went down, surfaced, gasped for air and gagged on silty water.

On the opposite riverbank, his companions saw what happened and ran alongside the river, trying to keep him in view. Jed soon slumped against a rock, out of breath. Lucinda's soggy dress made it hard for her to navigate the rocks and branches, so she flung it off on the dead run, while trying to keep her eye on Harriman, now just a head bobbing up and down in the river.

Rufus bounded over rocks. "Hold on, Mr. Hickenlooper, I'm coming!" He tripped and fell, but was up and running in a flash.

Harriman felt his arms and legs getting sluggish and going numb from cold and fear. The more he struggled to stay afloat, the more exhausted he got. Each time the current took him under his energy flagged and his panic grew. He was seeing not one elephant, but a herd of them. Scenes flashed before him—his parents sending him off to war, making it to the top of Mission Ridge, the bullet hole dead smack in the middle of Ridley's clock, the smiling face of the young Rebel spy he'd hung. He now saw his life slipping away down under the Ogeechee.

The water was murky and full of debris. He felt his lungs beginning to burst. He clawed and kicked the water in another frantic attempt to reach the surface. He was about to let it all go and breathe in his last when he heard a voice say:

"Stop fighting."

In one final superhuman effort, he willed his arms and legs to go limp. He forgot about his breath. Instead he felt a strange sense of well-being overtake him. Was this what dying was like? He stretched out his arms and glided through the water. It got shallower and he touched the river bottom with his feet. He pushed up and sucked in the cold air.

Ahead, he saw a fallen tree lodged between rocks in the rushing water. As he sped past the tree, he looped an arm around one of its outstretched branches. He drew in several more deep breaths and hung off the branch, letting his body sway in the current.

Rufus caught up to him and reached out a hand, gasping.

"What took you?"

"Are you all right, Mr. Hickenlooper?"

"Yes. And for God's sakes, call me Harriman."

CHAPTER 42

Diary entry of December 22nd, 1867

    *Who would have ever imagined that our companions would
be the sister of a Rebel boy Mr. Hickenlooper may have killed and a
former slave whose family he had involuntarily sent to their deaths?*

    *But here we are. And as we approach Savannah, we see more
and more people waiting by the side of the road, as if they've
been hoping the road past their door was the one we would take.
Sometimes they wave and cheer us on. Sometimes they are quiet
and reach out to touch Mr. Hickenlooper's flag. Sometimes they
curse and turn their backs on us.*

    *But by now it's clear even to Mr. Hickenlooper that the reason
they are there, friend or foe, is to see us. I even overheard a mother
tell her boy to remember what he saw. And, believe it or not, here
in Southeast Georgia, mostly they wish us well. Who would have
ever imagined?*

    Miss Rutledge finished reading the dispatch and put it on the
table. Jack Connolly stared out the window.

    "We run it tomorrow. We've not missed any, have we?"

"No, Mr. Connolly, not one." Irma Rutledge let a smile pass across her lips.

"What is it?"

"I'm glad you gave that boy a chance and ran these pieces. I'm not sure you are aware how much people want to know if he's still alive, who these other people on the journey are, what he sees. Honestly, the questions keep coming. They actually care how this all turns out."

"Actually, I am aware. They ask me the same questions. Even Ridley can't hide his curiosity."

Lucas Rawls approached the farmhouse and knocked on the door. After no response, he knocked again.

"Who's there?" a voice echoed from inside.

"It's me, Lucas."

Footsteps shuffled up. Eustis Hoffberger, one of the veterans who had been so enraged by Hickenlooper's bet at the reunion, glared from the crack in the door with his one good eye. "Heard you was making the rounds. What's a matter, don't ya got better things to do?"

"You gonna let me in?"

"You just stay there." Eustis went back inside and emerged a few moments later. "Pull up a chair. Want a pull?" he asked, offering a plug of tobacco.

"Don't touch the stuff anymore. Missus says it's like lickin' a spittoon."

"Can't have that, can we?" Eustis popped the plug in his mouth. "What's on yer mind?"

"The wager."

Eustis looked up expectantly. "Tell me somethin' new. What, he made it?"

"No, not yet." Lucas eyed the veteran, but he was thinking about something else. "You know what, Eustis?"

"No, what, Lucas?"

"I've been thinkin'."

"Uh-oh." Eustis leaned back in his chair, folded his hands behind his head and spat out a wad of tobacco juice.

CHAPTER 43

———⟶◦◦◦⟵———

They made it to Savannah at dusk on December 23rd, 1867. The city was festooned with Christmas bunting and decorations. It would have been quite different had Savannah met the fate of other places Sherman had passed through—Atlanta, Columbia, Eden, Griswoldville, all burned to the ground—but rumor had it that Uncle Billy had made friends with several Savannah ladies during his time as a railroad engineer before the war, and those friendships endured. You could say that Southern hospitality saved the city.

The travelers stopped in front of a large hotel. Lucinda was painfully aware of how disheveled she looked when she saw ladies in fine dresses eyeing her. Jed was conscious that people were staring at this strange group and felt the urge to disappear. Rufus was hungry.

"I lost my money in the river," Harriman said.

"Me too," Rufus said.

"Din't have none to lose," Jed shrugged.

Lucinda dug around in her dress, much to the consternation of passers-by. Conscious of their disapproving stares, she stepped into an alleyway. She came out clutching a sack of coins. "Seek and ya might find sumthin'."

Harriman rang the bell by the large leather register at the front desk. A clerk emerged from the back office and eyed the four travelers critically.

"I'd like four rooms, please."

"Sure," the clerk said, pushing the register forward. "If you'd sign in, please." Rufus wrote in their names. The clerk eyed the travelers' disheveled clothes, then noticed Jed standing behind them.

"He with you?"

Harriman nodded.

"I only have three rooms left." Another guest came up. "Excuse me," the clerk said, and reached behind him to a large rack of room keys hanging on hooks. There were more than four keys there.

"S'alright, I'll find me a place," Jed said.

"That's okay, we'll find somewhere else to stay," Harriman said and headed for the door.

"Suit yourself."

Rufus hung back.

"You stayin'?" the desk clerk asked.

Rufus turned the register around and pointed to Harriman Hickenlooper's name and address.

"It's him! The Yank from Iowa!" the desk clerk exclaimed.

"You know about him?" Rufus asked.

"Everyone knows who you are." The clerk pushed past Rufus and grabbed Harriman's hand. "Savannah's been betting on your march. Welcome, Mr. Hickenlooper."

"Bet? Another bet?" Lucinda asked.

"The bet." The clerk gestured quotation marks with his fingers. "Whether you'd make it here or not. Some thought you were nuts, some thought you were doing it for the money. Odds were you wouldn't get here."

"What did you think?" Harriman asked.

"If you made it, it meant you got treated right and folks up North might see we're still Americans. We lost the war, but we don't have to keep fightin' it." The clerk clapped his hands. "I just won me some money!"

"How much?" Lucinda asked.

"Two bucks."

"Well, since I've made you some money, how about you get us four rooms?"

"I'll see what I can do."

"Do that," Harriman answered, noticing Jed leave the lobby. "Hold on, Jed."

"S'okay, suh. No trouble. I'll find me a bed." He slipped out the door.

"Three rooms it is," the clerk said, grabbing room keys off their hooks.

"Where's the nearest telegraph office?" Rufus asked.

"Boy, take these bags and show our guests to 211, 212 and 213," the desk clerk barked at a black bellhop. "Telegraph's four blocks down, on Parish Street."

CHAPTER 44

Jack Connolly stood over the telegraph operator, reading Rufus's dispatch. He stuffed a banknote into the operator's shirt pocket. "Nobody hears about this until I say so."

The operator scowled as he wrote out the rest of the message clacking off the telegraph wire.

Connolly folded the dispatch in his coat, slapped his knee and headed straight for the Farmers and Mechanics Bank.

Walter Ridley was meeting with a customer. Connolly sat down and waited, watching Ridley smoothly conclude his business.

"Good day, Jack," said Ridley.

"Things going well, Walter?"

"Capital, capital."

"No pun intended," Connolly mused.

"Very good!" Ridley laughed and slapped Connolly's arm. "Going to have a good Christmas?"

"It'll be interesting. Listen, Walter. I thought you'd appreciate seeing this first. As a professional courtesy." Connolly handed the telegram to Ridley and walked over to the big glass window facing Main Street. As Ridley read the cable, Connolly watched him out of the corner of his eye.

"What an achievement!" Ridley exclaimed. He lowered his voice, as if there were people in the empty office. "Is this true? What is the source of this story?"

"I sent someone down there to cover the wager. You've been reading his dispatches, haven't you?" Connolly smiled. "I'd be offended if you hadn't."

"Of course I have. Who hasn't been reading *The Loyal Citizen* to get the latest? What I mean is, is this person reliable? Are there any other witnesses?"

"Rufus Dewes. He's not from here. Grew up in Ottumwa. He's a good young reporter. 'Georgia has swallowed Harriman Hickenlooper'. That's one of my favorites."

"Unh-hunh. I'm sure. Still, I have to ask how you know this is true?"

"Because it's my paper, he's my reporter and I stand behind every word." Connolly's voice was even and calm.

"That's noble, Jack, but I needn't remind you that Hickenlooper and I each have serious stakes in this wager. If, and only if, Hickenlooper walks into my office on or before the agreed-upon date and shows me solid evidence he was there, that's when I'll believe it."

"That's all true. But I was glad he made it. I mean, just that he's still alive. Aren't you?"

"Of course."

"Walter, you bought the Hickenlooper note from the bank."

"Yes."

"Was he in trouble?"

"The bank was going to have to foreclose on him eventually. Years ago the bank lent his parents the money to buy that farm, on my recommendation. I felt a special connection to it, and to the family."

"Is it unusual for a bank officer to purchase an asset from his own organization?"

"Appropriate question." Ridley fidgeted.

Connolly waited. "Is there an appropriate answer?"

"I thought I was doing the right thing for all concerned. The decision was taken by the Board of Directors. Everything was above board. I saved the bank the expense and awkwardness of a foreclosure on a troubled veteran. I spared Harry the humiliation and painful dislocation of losing his farm. Things like that rend a community. I would never foreclose on a fellow soldier with whom I shared the sacrifices of war."

"I wasn't suggesting that you would. But then, why did you make the bet, if, as you say, you have no intention of moving him off his farm in spite of him not making his payments? What do you win if you win, if you see what I mean?"

Ridley glared at Connolly, but his tone was cool and composed. "Jack, I don't have to explain to you that the war did a lot of damage to a lot of people, and the damage was not just physical. I cannot explain why Harry made this bet. I certainly cannot explain why Harry offered his farm as a stake for this bet. I can only explain that I saw a way to solve two problems at the same time. And if he wins the bet, that would be fine, too. Everyone deserves a second chance." Ridley glanced at his watch. "I will read the dispatches with greater interest, now that he is halfway home. Today is..." Ridley glanced at a wall calendar. "December 24th. He has a week. Good day, Jack."

Connolly nodded, tipped his hat and left.

Connolly reread Rufus's Savannah cable. The babbling outside disturbed him. He went to the door and overheard townspeople clamoring excitedly about Hickenlooper's arrival in Savannah. *Curse that damned telegraph operator. Waste of a good bribe,* Connolly thought.

Miss Rutledge walked in and sat down by Connolly's desk. "Henry Garber is in town."

"Our esteemed congressman? What does he want?"

"He asked me if he might have a word with you. I told him you would be back around now. He is staying at the Mayflower Hotel. Shall I tell him you will meet with him?"

Connolly nodded.

Miss Rutledge gathered her coat and hat. "I left his latest letter on your desk."

"I saw that." Connolly scowled. "What'd it say?"

"He seems to have been following the march in *The Loyal Citizen* more closely. You might want to read it before you meet him."

"Fine." Connolly took the letter, scanned the first few sentences impatiently as he paced about the room, then stopped and sat down. His nostrils flared and his face turned red. "The hell you say!"

The bell above the door tinkled. Miss Rutledge led Henry Garber, distinguished Unites States congressman from the 2nd district of Iowa, into Connolly's office.

"Henry Garber. What a pleasant surprise. Come in. What can I do for you?"

Henry Garber had the look of a man whose steel-rimmed glasses, fine suit and honorable title could not disguise his fundamental unease with the way he found the world. Today was no exception.

"Do you have any tonic?"

"Miss Rutledge, do we have any tonic?"

Garber fidgeted in his chair. Not usually lost for words, he wasn't finding them easily now.

"C'mon, Henry, cat got your tongue?"

"Did you receive my letter, Jack?"

"I did."

Irma returned with Garber's drink and sat down at her desk. Garber eyed her nervously.

"Miss Rutledge, would you excuse us, please?"

"Of course."

"Come on, Jack, let's not play around here. Did you read my letter?"

"Yes."

Garber sighed, waiting for further clarification. None came.

"Can we speak plainly here?"

"Off the record, you mean?"

Garber nodded. "I don't think you appreciate the pressure I am under."

"No, I don't think I do. Enlighten me."

"Let me paint you a picture of what's going on in Washington. The Democrats support Johnson and want our troops out of the South as soon as possible so they can revive the cotton and tobacco-growing businesses that benefit New York exporters. Johnson says the Congress has a duty to uphold his Reconstruction policies. Congress disagrees, and wants to dictate policy to him. Stanton, Johnson's own Secretary of War, is more hostile to the president every day. He wants the army to stay in the South and enforce these new civil rights laws for the blacks. The other day he actually refused to leave his office and locked himself inside for fear he'd be sacked by Johnson and locked out of it. The Radical Republicans are hell-bent on giving blacks voting rights, property rights, and using the army to make sure they get them. They claim those people are being lynched and are demanding that the army protect freed slaves. General Grant keeps his presidential options open while commanding the occupied South with Union Armies. Southerners seethe under this occupation and harbor a deep desire to exact revenge on the people that were supposedly freed by the war. Republicans openly hope Grant will run against Johnson in '68. He will win. Johnson vetoes Republican bills. The Republicans override Johnson. It's a mess." Garber drained the tonic in a few gulps.

Connolly eyed the congressman. "I don't see what the pressure is for you in all this."

"Everyone thought Appomattox ended the war. The fighting hasn't stopped. People just use harsh words, public opinion and parliamentary procedures instead of guns. But mark my words, it could explode again. There is no middle ground."

Connolly picked up Garber's letter and read out loud:

"'...specifically the possible 'implications' this story might have on the debates currently taking place in the capitol on the tender subjects of Reconstruction, national unity and impeachment...

Mr. Hickenlooper's journey perceived as symbolic of a national need for reunification... desire to see this perception handled carefully...' You ask me to consider the dangers this story could have on the impeachment debate." He looked up. "I understand that you feel the disagreements are explosive. That's probably a good cue to warn people and tell them what's really going on, don't you think? Let them see what the stakes are in this fight. I am not a good enough reporter to predict the impact of this story."

"Horseshit, you aren't!" Garber sucked on his tonic, loosened his tie and drew on an empty glass, slamming it on the desk. "Who're you talking to, Jim? We go back a long time. Mrs. Roberts' sixth grade, to be exact. You're the editor. You run stories to sell newspapers. Controversy makes good stories. This fool is stirring things up where they ought not be stirred up any more than they already are. Don't add fuel to this fire. What he's doing is, it's irresponsible. And you ought to know that."

"I don't see it like that, Henry."

"Oh, really?"

"People call him crazy. You say irresponsible. What's crazy about wanting to heal from the war? Besides, it's too late."

"What? Why?"

"He made it to Savannah."

Garber sat down. "Well, I'll be." He could not disguise his amazement, then remembered his outrage. "So do I understand you correctly, that there is nothing you can do about this story?"

"I can't bury history, and neither can you, Henry. What he's doing in Georgia, what you're facing in Washington, D.C., it's all the same story. I still have to take a stab at describing it." Connolly pushed his glasses to his forehead. "Let me ask you something. If the Republicans impeach Johnson, how will you vote?"

"If it comes to that, you'll read about it. In the Burlington Sentinel. I think you've made a mistake here, Jack, one you can't walk back from. Good day to you."

"Merry Christmas, Henry." The bells above the door tinkled.

Miss Rutledge crossed paths with Henry Garber and slid quickly inside as the door slammed behind her. "He didn't look too pleased."

"I should have spiked his drink."

"Would it have helped?"

Connolly shook his head and eyed Garber's letter lying on the desk. "Miss Rutledge, did I ever tell you that if there is one thing I cannot stand, it's politicians telling me what I should or should not write."

"More than once, Mr. Connolly. They're on your head."

Connolly felt for his glasses and slipped them on. He scanned Garber's letter again, crumpled it and dropkicked it in the trash.

CHAPTER 45

Harriman and Lucinda walked the streets of Savannah for
hours at a time. Lucinda was especially taken with the
squares—Oglethorpe, Orleans, Chippewa, Ellis, Columbia—
that interlaced the city. The waterfront showcased numerous
tall ships loading and unloading cargo from all over the world.
In short, Savannah presented a picture of a world they could
scarcely imagine, yet was now right in front of them, and one
that, amazingly, welcomed them with open arms. People stopped
them on the street and asked questions about their journey.
Occasionally folks would see them coming and cross the street or
turn their backs.

On Christmas Eve day, they returned to the hotel from their
customary walk and were met by a detachment of Union soldiers
standing outside, cordoning off a crowd of people. A young officer
stepped forward.

"Harriman Hickenlooper?"

"Yes."

"Lieutenant Rodney Lewis. And you are?"

"Lucinda McWhorter."

Lewis touched the brim of his cap. "Mr. Hickenlooper, on behalf of the Military Commander of the District of Georgia, I am pleased to offer you a military escort during your stay in Savannah. How long do you plan to be here?"

"Why?"

Lieutenant Lewis sighed and surveyed the crowd listening in on their conversation. He pulled Harriman off to the side and spoke in a low tone. "Do you realize, sir, any one of these people might try to kill you?"

Harriman eyed the young lieutenant, so eager to do his duty and serious in his intent. "Lieutenant, people tried to kill me for years, so it doesn't get to me like it used to. The truth is, the best protection I have ever, or will ever have, comes from the good Lord. Common sense and decency help. I can't accept your offer."

Lucinda elbowed him.

"What?"

"Maybe he's right."

"If someone wants to kill me, they're going to try. Besides, the bet says I may only rely on the good will of whoever I meet."

"Praise the Lord!" someone called out.

"Suit yourself. Good day, miss. Company, fall in!"

"Merry Christmas, Lieutenant," Harriman called out.

The crowd parted for the soldiers amid applause and some catcalls.

At the telegraph office, Rufus was reading Connolly's comments scribbled on a copy of the latest piece he'd sent in about the color bearer's arrival. He also appreciated the wired money the editor had included. He almost missed the postscript at the bottom of the page commending him on his instincts for the story and the courage he showed following them. The editor's praise made him happier than the money did. The fact that they had enough time to make it home and win the bet made him happiest of all.

Harriman and Lucinda ate a quiet dinner in her room. When they were finished, she patted the bed for him to come join her. He took her hand.

"Come with me tomorrow."

"I can't. It ain't where I belong. Iowa's the moon to me. I'd never fit in there." She caressed his cheek. "Ya know it, too."

"I'll stay here then."

"Ya can't do that. The bet…"

"I lost it the moment I met you. The bet says I have to return 'untouched'. You touched me, all the way deep in here. I want you to be with me until the day I die." He took her hand and pressed it to his cheek, then gathered her up in his arms. He kissed her, softly at first. His mouth traced her lips, her eyes, into all the delicate places. First their fingers, then their bodies curled to each other. She felt him harden and she for an instant imagined what he would feel like inside her. The thought warmed, excited and scared her all at once.

He took her hand to guide it between his legs.

"No. We go there, it'll make the partin' even worse." She sighed, grasped his hand and kissed it. When he fell asleep, she took him close in her arms.

It was the light of the full moon streaming through the window that awakened him, still wrapped in her arms.

"Say yes. Please," he whispered in her ear.

She stirred. "I can't. I wouldn't fit in."

"You fit in with me anywhere."

"It ain't you, don't ya see? Every time I'd walk down the street, I'd be the enemy that took away their sons, brothers an' fathers. I'm the enemy took your brother away."

"People are talking about this country like it's two countries, forever apart. I can't accept that my brother and how many others died for *nothing!* You and I don't belong in Georgia or Iowa. We belong here." He pounded on his heart and kissed her. "We can go west, make a new start."

"An' give up yer farm fer nuthin."

"Not for nothing. For you."

"I can't! I won't. You saw how them fancy Savannah ladies stared down at me. No? Well, I did. Who'm I foolin'? I'm a backwoods girl who cain't read or write a lick. I got the clothes on my back an' a pistol in my pocket. I'm nuthin' here, and this is my country. What'd I be in yours?"

"It's *our* country."

She stroked his cheek. "I know you believe that, heart n' soul." She rose from the bed and went to the window. Moonlight sparkled on the tears running down her face. "There's been too much blood."

He got up and stood behind her, gazing up at the moon with her. "I don't want you to come and see me off tomorrow. We'll say goodbye now." Harriman leaned over and kissed her lightly on her quivering lips, then at the tears running down her cheeks. "I'll always love you, Lucinda." He softly closed the door behind him.

"I'll always love you, too," she whispered to no one.

CHAPTER 46

A crowd had gathered at the train station in a drizzling rain.
Placards, some crude, some ornate, announced that well-
wishers were here to wish Harriman on his way. A few signs read
things like "YANKEE GO HOME," or "GOOD RIDDANCE,"
but it was clear that the city of Savannah wanted a good send-off
for the color bearer.

Harriman made his way through the throng of people,
shaking hands.

Rufus and Jed followed behind him. "Where's Lucinda?" Rufus
asked, looking around.

He waved and scanned the crowd. He caught sight of her in the
sea of faces, moving steadily through the crowd. He jumped off the
platform, pushing his way through people to get to her. They met in
the middle of the crowd.

"I told you not to come."

"I had to." They embraced.

The whistle blew and the conductor called out, "All aboard!"

A figure emerged through the crowd.

Harriman recognized the figure. "I have something for you," he said as he brandished Red's red bandanna that he had carried in his pocket since their fight at the river.

"Got somethin' fer you, too." Red said and lunged at Harriman.

"No!" Lucinda screamed and threw herself in front of Harriman. Red's knife caught her in her side. She groaned and collapsed to the ground. Rufus lunged at Red but someone got between them and knocked him down. The man pulled a pistol, waved it in his face and snarled, "Let him go, kid." It was Miles Brockenbrough, the traveling salesman they had met on the train in Chattanooga, the man with "all the friends Harriman would ever need." Brockenbrough fired his pistol in the air. The shot scattered the crowd. "Follow me!" he grabbed Red. They ducked into an alley and disappeared before anyone could give chase.

"Get a doctor!" Harriman shouted as he cradled Lucinda in his arms. He stanched the blood flowing out of the wound in her side with Red's bandanna. A man bent down next to him.

"I'm a doctor. There's a hospital not far from here," the man said. "We can take my buggy. Come." They carried Lucinda to the buggy.

The train whistle blew. The train pulled out of the station as people trailed off in the rain.

Harriman knocked. A nurse opened the door.

"May I see her?"

"She's in the bed at the end, on the left. Best not to stay too long. She's weak, and very lucky."

"Thanks, ma'am," Harriman said. As he walked down the center aisle of the hospital ward, he noticed the large number of maimed and disfigured young men staring at him.

"What happened to ya, missy?" an amputee lying in the next bed was asking Lucinda.

"Stopped a knife." Lucinda shrugged, winced, then saw Harriman. "They catch 'em?"

"No." He placed a package on the bed. "Merry Christmas." He opened it for her. The aroma of freshly-baked bread filled the room. Harriman broke off a piece and handed it to Lucinda. She took a bite, then saw the amputee's hungry gaze and gave it to him.

"Is it Christmas?"

"Two days ago. Once they got you sewed up, you slept clean through to now. The knife missed some important parts by inches."

"My Christmas present, my life."

"You came to the station. Why?"

"I had to see you again. I bet Iowa's cold, right? Colder than Georgia."

"Yes." He caught her drift and kissed her.

She chewed on the bread, watching the amputee devour his. Tears welled up in her eyes.

"What's wrong?"

"Y'ain't gonna make it it back in time."

"No matter." Harriman was so close his face was almost touching hers. "Everything I ever wanted is looking up at me right now. Don't fret. Will you marry me?"

"Two promises. They're easy, an' I know how good you are at keepin' em'."

"Thank you."

"Y'ain't heard 'em yet."

He nodded.

"One, we get married here in Savannah."

"Agreed."

"Two. Gotta have special rings. An' you make no more bets."

"That's three things," Rufus interjected, depositing gifts from well-wishers next to the bed.

"Too bad," they answered back.

"I have a condition," Harriman said, turning to her.

"Mmm?"

"We do it today."

"Today? Cain't get outta bed, can't get married. Got no ring, neither."

"Mr. Dewes."

"Yes, Mr. Hickenlooper?"

"Mr. Dewes, we need your help."

"Anything, Mr. Hickenlooper. Name it."

"Find us a preacher."

"An' a blacksmith," Lucinda said.

"Hunh?" Harriman and Rufus answered.

"It's the bread." The amputee shrugged, savoring another bite.

They gathered around her hospital bed. Harriman stood beside Lucinda. Patients, doctors and nurses formed a ring of witnesses.

The preacher was clearly nervous performing his duty under the circumstances. "Do you have the rings?"

"Sure do." Rufus stepped forward and handed him a small package.

The preacher unwrapped the package and did a double take at what he saw. There were two wedding rings there but looking closer, the preacher recognized rifling grooves in the bands. It took him a moment to figure out that he was looking at rings made from rifle bullets. He cleared his throat. "Uh, will you wear these rings as symbols of your union?"

"We will."

"Then, by the grace of God, I now pronounce you man and wife."

Later that night, Jed entered the ward. Harriman slept at the foot of Lucinda's bed.

"Congratulations, Miss Lucinda. I's happy for you. How you feelin'?"

"Best day of my life. And it's my birthday, too. Missed you at the wedding."

Harriman stirred and sat up. "Yes, we did."

"The folks run dis place din't see it dat way. No matter, I's here now. How old you be, girl?"

"Seventeen."

"Happy birthday."

"How old are you, Jed?" Harriman asked.

"Couldn't tell ya, and don't care to count. But goin' to Sea Island got me feelin' I's young again, dat dere's sumpin' left to this life."

"You're really going to Sea Island?" Harriman asked.

Jed nodded. "Yup. Mistuh Rufus got me a map. Can't get lost now." He grimaced a smile. "Best be goin', 'fore they find out I's here."

"You take care of yourself, Jed," Harriman said.

"Good Lord do dat for me. Been a privlige, suh."

"For me, too. And thank you, Jed."

"Fer what?"

"For forgiving me."

"What I know 'bout you, suh, you'd sherly do the same." For the first time in his life, Jed shook a white man's hand. He turned and walked out. His footsteps mingled with the sounds of broken men snoring in their beds.

Rufus sat at the small table in his hotel room, staring out the window into the darkened Savannah street. He started to write, then crumpled the page and threw it on the floor, where it fell into a pile of other crumpled pages.

Sure, the color bearer had made it to Savannah. But after all they'd been through, his triumph was tragic. When the girl put herself in front of that knife and saved the color bearer's life, she ensured that he lost everything he had.

He heard Connolly's voice inside his head. "Stay on the story, wherever it goes."

The date on his diary entry read December 28th. He looked at his watch. It was almost the 29th. He began to write the dispatch.

CHAPTER 47

D ecember 30th was cold and clear. Connolly went through his usual routine—tending to his wife, feeding the cats, reviewing his list of things to do that day—and set out for his usual walk to *The Loyal Citizen* office.

To his surprise, the telegraph operator was waiting for him when he arrived. "Thought you'd like to see this first thing."

Connolly nodded and felt in his pocket for some change.

"No charge." Before he could ask why, the telegraph operator turned and walked away.

Strange. That man doesn't take a breath for free, he thought.

Connolly read the cable and entered the office.

Irma Rutledge reacted to the scowl on his face. "Are you all right, Mr. Connolly? Bad news?"

"He won't get back in time. Seems he went and fell in love with some Rebel girl. Married her. We're going to a second edition today." He handed her the cable, went into his office and closed the door.

Walter Ridley listened as Louise read the dispatch in the paper out loud. When she had finished, he let out an audible sigh. Of course, he'd read and savored it twice before, but he wanted his wife to think she was reading it to him for the first time.

"What are you so upset about?" she asked.

"Don't you think it's sad this young man went to such extreme lengths to make a point and lost everything proving it?"

"It says here that the girl he married was the sister of a boy he killed. How astonishing."

"The whole thing is insane."

"Ever the romantic, aren't you, Walter?"

Ridley shrugged. "I needn't remind you, Louise, that whatever I lack in romance is more than made up for by the additional property we now own."

Sweeter than their increase in wealth was the deeply satisfying revenge that was his alone.

CHAPTER 48

The train wended its way north. Whenever it made a stop for water or wood, Lucinda made a point of getting off to pick up mementos or talk to people waiting at the stations. It seemed to hasten her recovery and increase her strength to soak up the sights, smells and scenes of a new country. Seeing this delighted Harriman to no end.

Rufus wrote dispatches and telegraphed them wherever he could, all the while keeping his diary current. Somewhere along the journey, he had started a scrapbook. One thing was missing.

Harriman had still not given him an interview. He had also made Rufus agree not to send any more dispatches once they crossed into Illinois. He wanted no Iowa crowds meeting them before they got home.

"Next stop, Springfield. Springfield, Illinois, next stop. Please watch your step getting off the train," the conductor announced.

Harriman rose, gathered his things and headed for the end of the car.

"This isn't our stop," Rufus said.

"What else is new? C'mon, 'fore he finds trouble," Lucinda said.

Harriman asked directions only once, and out of earshot of his fellow travelers. They arrived at a cast-iron archway that said 'OAK RIDGE CEMETERY'. The place was deserted, except for a couple of black caretakers sweeping the walkways. Harriman stopped one of the caretakers and again asked something out of earshot of his companions.

They made their way to a crypt built into the side of a gentle knoll. There, Harriman bowed his head before a small plaque to the side of the large iron doors. The plaque read: ABRAHAM LINCOLN, 1809—1865.

"I still can't believe they killed him," Rufus said.

"Who?" Lucinda asked.

"Abraham Lincoln,' Harriman answered, pointing at the plaque.

"Oh." Lucinda walked off.

"I can," Harriman said.

"Why? I thought you loved Mr. Lincoln," Rufus said.

"I do. Love cuts both ways."

"I don't understand," Rufus said.

Harriman sat down on a bench near the crypt, staring at the other gravestones, listening to the sound of the caretaker's broom sweeping on stone. "It was Easter time. The fourth spring of the war. We'd beaten Joe Johnston's army at Bentonville, and were chasing what was left of it around North Carolina. We'd heard that Lee was close to surrendering. We knew it was over. Everyone felt this immense thrill of victory." Harriman paused. "There wasn't a man among us that wasn't terrified of being the last one to die either.

"We entered this town, and like most other towns, there was no one in sight when we arrived. We were relaxed, almost kidding around. Bugler sounded assembly and we formed up in the town square. Ridley read an announcement." Again, he paused and sighed.

"Ridley said that President Lincoln had been shot and died on Good Friday. We couldn't believe it. He also said some Rebs had tried to kill the rest of the Cabinet, but had failed and some of the assassins were still on the loose. The boys were ready to torch the town right then. Ridley reminded us we had strict orders to maintain security and act like soldiers."

Lucinda had returned and stood listening nearby, as was the black caretaker.

"Ridley said that General Sherman had ordered black bunting hung from every window in every town we came through to show our grief and respect for our fallen president. The quartermasters gave out rolls of the stuff. Lucas and me got to this one house and knocked on the door.

"At first, no one answered. I knew someone was home, I'd seen a face peer out from a window curtain. 'Open the goddamned door, you dirty Rebel.' I was about to beat the door down when it swung open. The woman standing there didn't look right."

"What do you mean, din't look right?" Lucinda asked.

"I mean, I could see she was young by how smooth and unwrinkled her skin was. But her hair was white, white as snow. She wore a black dress, like she'd been to a funeral. I was so surprised I forgot why I was there for a minute.

"Lucas told her we had orders to hang this stuff from her balcony, as a sign of respect and mourning for our president. And she answered, 'He is not my president.' I swear to God, I almost shot her right there. I told her we had orders to burn her house down if she did not comply.

"'This is an outrage,' she said.

"'Killing President Lincoln just when this war's done, that's the outrage!' I shouted.

"Her face turned the color of her hair. She grabbed my sleeve. 'I have given a husband and a brother for our cause. Please, I beseech you. I will do as you order, but please leave my house. Leave me my dignity.'

"I realized she had not heard the news. 'Hurry it up. We'll be watching.'

"The woman walked out onto her balcony overlooking the street, carrying a roll of bunting under her arm. Some of the boys were yelling at her and catcalling. The woman ignored them and carefully wrapped the cotton bunting around the metal grating, then wrapped it around her neck. She mounted the railing, looked me in the eye and without missing a beat, dropped off. Just. Like. That. Everyone got real quiet. Ridley ordered me to cut her down."

"Lord have mercy," the caretaker mumbled. He crossed himself and moved off.

Lucinda held her mouth over her hand.

Rufus wrote.

"She loved her cause as deeply as I loved my president," Harriman said. "And she gave her life for it, even after it was lost. It cuts both ways." He gazed at the crypt. "I think of him as the last to die."

CHAPTER 49

B urton Ball gazed out the window of his study. He saw Red walking up the steps and heard him knock on the door. Footsteps echoed, and Ball heard his servant's protests downstairs. Red and a new servant appeared at the door to Ball's office. The servant started to explain how Red got past him, but Ball waved him away. "Did you find Jed?"

Red nodded.

"Well? Where is he? Did you bring him back. You didn't, did you?"

Red moved into the room, never taking his eyes off Ball. "I never figgered I'd hate anything worse than a bluebelly. But I do now. It's the lyin' coward I'm lookin at."

"What are you talking about?"

Red raised a hand and winced at the pain from his broken ribs. "Don' bother. Yer nigger wasn't stole. He run off." Red pulled out a pistol and aimed it between Ball's eyes. "I want the rest of my money."

"Absolutely not. Our agreement was that you got some on commencement of the task and the balance when you completed it. You didn't complete it. So you aren't getting it."

Red's eyebrows arched. "So yer not as big a coward as I thought you were." He pistol-whipped Ball across the face, opening a bloody gash. Ball rocked backwards and crashed onto the floor. Red was on him instantly. "Where's the rest of my money? You don't cough it up, I'll tear this place apart, an if'n I don't find it, I'll kill ya just to watch you die."

"You'll kill me anyway," Ball answered, blinded by the blood clouding his eyes.

"Ya think? Open yer lyin' mouth. Open it!"

Ball complied.

Red shoved the barrel in his mouth and cocked the hammer. "Where's the money?"

Ball gestured with half-crazed eyes to a shelf behind him. Red dismounted Ball and, keeping his pistol trained on him, rummaged around until he found a leather-bound box tucked behind the books. Inside were several stacks of greenbacks and assorted documents. He threw the books on the floor and grabbed the box.

A voice called from outside the door, "Everythin' okay, massuh?"

"Fine, fine. I'll call if I need anything." Ball managed to sound halfway persuasive, wiping blood from his face.

"Good at orders, ain't ya?" Red pulled some bills from the box and put the box on the shelf. "I oughtta take it all, you sack'a squirrel shit."

Ball inched his way toward his desk.

Red's eyes lit up as he counted the hoard of cash. He caught the reflection of the planter's movement in the portrait of Ball's grandfather Linus and just ducked away from the bullet from Ball's derringer, which smashed Linus to pieces.

Red whirled and shot Ball once, then two more times. Red first pocketed what he was owed, then what was left in the box and stepped over Ball. Downstairs, Red encountered the servant, who saw the gun in his hand and backed away.

"Go on an' get some a' that freedom, boy. It's on me!" Red said. He fired a shot into the chandelier above the petrified boy's head and stormed out the door.

CHAPTER 50

They arrived in Centerville on a cold, gray morning just before dawn on the 21st of January, 1868. They walked onto Main Street as a light snow began to fall.

"Ain't never seen it before," said Lucinda, reaching out and tasting the white flakes that settled in her hand.

"Aw, c'mon. You're joking, right?" Rufus asked.

Harriman looked down the street and closed his eyes. "All through the war, I dreamed of the day when I would walk in a parade down this street with my brother by my side. There'd be bands playing and people cheering. The big one wasn't like that."

"S'kinda quiet," Lucinda said, smiling and holding onto his arm as they walked down the empty street, which was slowly revealing itself in the dawn's light.

"Are you talking about the review of the Grand Army of the Republic?" Rufus asked.

Harriman nodded. "We arrived in Washington up from the Carolinas in late May. The place was so full of soldiers, we had to camp in people's yards. The Army of the Potomac got to march first, I guess because they got most of the attention, going back and forth between

Washington and Richmond the whole time. What's that, a hundred miles? We campaigned two thousand miles from Illinois through Mississippi, Tennessee , Georgia, South Carolina and North Carolina."

A sleepy head peered out from behind a window-shade. They continued down the street.

"On the second day, we got our turn. General Sherman rode to the head of the column, took off his hat, and led all 75,000 of us in the Army of the Tennessee down Pennsylvania Avenue past where President Johnson and General Grant, and all the important people were sitting. When I saw President Johnson there, I felt cheated. Lincoln should have been sitting there, sharing our victory. He carried us to the end." He choked up and turned away. She waited for him until he was able to walk on. "As we marched by, I looked down our line and names and faces came pouring back to me. Norville Ruley at Shiloh. Billy Brockleiter at Big Black River. Silas Etheridge at Kennesaw Mountain. All three McClintock brothers—David, William and Warren—in the Vicksburg siege lines. Reuben Badeau at New Hope Church. Damon Granger at Griswoldville, Alonzo Hickenlooper at Eden. Abraham Lincoln in Washington, D.C.

"It should have been a happy day, but it wasn't a parade, it was a funeral. The dead won the war the hardest way. They gave up everything."

Lucinda stopped and took him in her arms. "Don't you git it? Their sufferin's over. The hardest way is fer the ones they left behind. It's you, an' me, an' Rufus, all of us, we're the ones got to make good on the debt we owe them. We owe it to them to make the world better'n we found it. I don't never fergit that. An' you ain't, neither."

"What I'm trying to say is, you and me, right this moment, this is better than any parade I ever wanted to be in... I do love you so."

"I know you do. I love you, too."

They kissed long and deep.

Rufus put his notebook back in his pocket and kept walking.

Some people woke up that cold morning in the first month of 1868 and when they looked outside, they saw three people walking down the street. They recognized the color bearer, they might have recognized the kid, but they surely didn't recognize the girl with her arms around Hickenlooper, kissing him under a falling snow that covered them in a fine white blanket.

The news that Hickenlooper had returned spread fast. The town elders, Ridley foremost amongst them, organized a town meeting.

On January 22nd, the town hall was packed to the rafters. When there was no more room, people spilled out into the snow-covered street and demanded the doors be left open so they could hear what went on inside. Ridley arrived and worked his way through the crowd to the platform. Lucas Rawls was there. So was Jakob Dreisler, the neighbor who had bought Harriman's cow. The one-eyed veteran Eustis Hoffberger was there. Almost all of the Sixth Iowa was there. Jack Connolly stood with Rufus and Miss Rutledge in the back of the room.

There was a commotion outside and a growing cacophony of voices. Harriman and Lucinda entered to cheers, a few boos, and some silent stares as people saw the girl for the first time. Comments ran the gauntlet from, "Never thought you'd make it," "We were with you all the way," "Who's that with ya, hunh?" to "Why'd ya come back, Rebel lover?" Some men reached out and clapped him on the back. Harriman carried the walking stick and flag over his shoulder. They made their way to the front of the room and sat down in the first row.

Ridley raised his hands for quiet and turned to Harriman. "You have accomplished something I, and perhaps most of the people in this room, didn't think was possible. You have come through it untouched. We are all proud of you and grateful you have returned. Personally, I am pleasantly surprised to see you with such a lovely companion."

Dewes nudged Connolly. "This is such horseshit."

"There's a lad," Connolly smiled.

"Please introduce her to us," Ridley said.

Harriman rose and gestured for Lucinda to rise as well. She stayed glued to her chair.

"I want to thank everyone for coming here to welcome my wife and me. Her name is Lucinda."

"Congratulations. Let's have three cheers for Harriman and his new bride. Hip, hip…"

"What about the bet?" someone shouted.

"These folks must be tired from their long journey. There will be time to discuss that later."

"No, that's the question." Harriman turned to the room. "I was to go unarmed and return by New Year's Day, untouched. Well, it's well past New Year's Day, and I have been touched. Deeply touched. So I haven't met the terms of the bet." He took Lucinda's hand and sat down.

"I'd like to say somethin'," Lucas said, rising to his feet. "Har, like most folks, I couldn't figure out why you done this. Tried to talk you out of it. Tried to get the whole thing called off." He looked at Ridley. "Between worrying 'bout you and disagreein' with you, it kinda drove me crazy. But I kept thinkin' 'bout what you said, 'bout us all still bein' Americans and needin' to fergive each other." He nodded at Lucinda. "I remembered what you said 'bout if we fought to keep our country together, why are we acting like we got to keep it apart? I thought 'bout what kind of country I wanted to live in, the one that holds a grudge, or the one that gives people a second chance. That maybe when you give somebody a second chance, you're givin' yourself one, too. I'm not just glad you came back, Har. I'm proud of you."

"Hear, hear," someone called out.

"I ain't finished." Lucas turned to Ridley. "Comin' home with someone he's found to share his life with, it seems all the more fittin' he get a second chance. Wouldn't you agree?"

Ridley nodded.

"So, Colonel, some of us, we pooled our money and are askin' if we could pay off the note on Har's farm."

Harriman whirled around in his chair.

Ridley's jaw dropped.

"I'll be damned," Connolly said, elbowing Dewes so hard it knocked the pencil and pad out of his hands.

"Think on it, Colonel. We don't expect ya to give us an answer right now." Lucas sat down.

"That's a generous gesture. I will certainly consider it," Ridley replied.

"No need to," Harriman said. "I can't accept it, Lucas. You've all sacrificed as much as I me, some of you more…"

"Oh, no," Connolly groaned.

Lucinda gave Harriman a discreet but firm tug and pulled him down to her. "Ever heard that sayin', don't look a gift horse in the mouth?" she whispered, smiling sweetly. "Best accept it, sit down and shush."

Harriman straightened his coat. "I humbly accept your gift," Harriman said stiffly and sat down.

"First sane thing the man's done yet," Connolly said.

Someone yelled "HIP! HIP!" The room answered back, "HOORAY!" The cheers rolled across the room, billowed through the halls and poured out into the street, drowning out a smattering of boos and catcalls.

Ridley did not even try to quiet the cheering crowd.

CHAPTER 51

"Come in."

Harriman entered the plush, wood-paneled study. Noting the sound of ticking clocks in almost perfect syncopation, he sat down in a leather chair in front of Ridley's desk.

Ridley did not look up, but stayed focused on the papers in front of him.

Harriman reached into his saddlebag and pulled out a bulging envelope. He slid it across the desk. "Payment on the note. The boys wanted me to deliver it to you."

"How touching."

"And two copies of a release."

Ridley looked at the envelope, then got up and went to one of the clocks. He rubbed the glass on its face. "You seem very confident I will agree to this. What makes you think I will? I don't have to, you know."

"No, you don't. But you will."

"How's that?"

"Smart politics."

"I see." Ridley slapped the envelope in the palm of his hand, weighing it. He opened a drawer and withdrew a ledger. Reading from the ledger, he moistened his fingers and slowly counted out each bill in the envelope. When he was finished, he entered figures in the ledger, closed it and put it back in the drawer.

"Sign them," Harriman said, pushing the releases across the desk.

Ridley read the releases and signed them. "There."

"All right. We're finished here."

"Oh no, we are not. Aren't you forgetting something? One of the conditions of the bet was that you bring me solid evidence you made the march."

"Marrying Lucinda wasn't enough?"

"No."

"Do you remember I once told you I would square our accounts one day?"

"No, I can't recall as I do." Ridley opened a desk drawer, withdrew a small pistol and held it in his lap.

Harriman went to the mantel and reached into his bag.

Ridley cocked the pistol.

Harriman withdrew a battered clock with a bullet hole in the center of its face. He moved a pristine clock aside and placed the shot clock on the mantel, dead center. While Ridley gaped at the clock, Harriman carefully pulled out one bill, then another, from the wad of money on the desk and stuffed the bills in his pocket.

"That's twenty dollars. I believe the figure we agreed to was ten," Ridley said.

"Each."

Moments later, Louise Ridley entered the parlor. "Who was that? Are you all right, Walter? You look like you've seen a ghost."

What she saw was Walter Ridley staring at something on the mantel, a pistol and a wad of money on the desk in front of him.

Louise followed his gaze to the mantel. "What in God's name is that?"

For the second time in as many days, Walter Ridley could not find the words.

CHAPTER 52

Three Years Later

Harriman sat across from Rufus, turning a book over and over in his hands. He examined the cover, reading aloud: "'The Ones They Left Behind—Small Scenes from the Big Show, by Rufus Dewes.' I know him."

"I owe it to you."

"Why do you say that? You don't. You owe it to Jack Connolly."

"You took me along."

A dog barked, then ran into the room and jumped on Harriman's lap.

"Sorry, Mr. Hickenlooper. He got a mind'a his own. Smoke, git down now."

"It's okay." Harriman stroked Smoke, who nestled into his lap.

"Mr. Dewes!" Jed grimaced a smile.

"Jed! I don't believe it. How'd you get here?"

"Well, Mr. Dewes, I made it to Sea Island after all. An' it was jes' as you said. At first guvmint lent us land to work an' mules to work it, sayin' we could work to pay it off. We had schools, teachers. I learned to read and write. We even elected our own folks to make things run. But after a while, guvmint started breakin' promises. The white plantation owners didn't take to us havin' land a' our own and havin' a vote and a say-so on things. Eventually, folks started goin' north or back to the plantations. I wasn't doin' that, and wrote Mr. Harriman. He wrote me back tellin' me what he was doin', askin' me if I wanted to help out. Here I am."

"That's wonderful."

"He pays me, too."

"Well then, Jed, please tell Lucinda the wagon will be here any minute and assemble the others for Welcoming. Down, Smoke."

"I'll see it's done." Jed nodded. He spied the book Harriman held up and read the cover. "Congratulations, Mr. Dewes. You can quote me."

"You too, Jed." Rufus gazed after Smoke and the ex-slave and smiled. "Imagine that, Mr. Hickenlooper."

"Harriman to you."

Rufus smiled. "I thought you hated dogs."

Harriman shrugged. "Not this one."

"How is Mr. Connolly these days? I fell out of touch with him when I moved to Chicago."

"His wife died. He left town."

"Oh, I am sorry to hear that."

"I heard he settled in California somewhere and has a paper out there. Irma Rutledge runs *The Loyal Citizen* now. You should pay her a visit while you're here."

"I will. And the esteemed Walter Ridley?"

Harriman sighed. "He may be our next governor. He seems to think so, anyway."

"I'm not so sure. Now that my book is out, he may have some explaining to do."

"He's good at that. We would like you to stay for supper."

"Well, yes, of course I will."

They sat around a large table bedecked with fixings fit for their special guest. When they had all settled into their chairs, Harriman reached one hand to Lucinda and one to Jed. Jed clasped it and took Rufus's hand in his, forming a circle. Harriman smiled and bowed his head. "Dear God, thank you for giving me this day and this meal to share my truth, sadness, joy, wisdom and love with the people who mean the most to me in this world."

All held the moment solemnly except Rufus, who peeked to see when everyone else opened their eyes.

Jed brought out a plate of grits and pork chops and set it in front of Rufus. Sitting on the plate was a child's toy elephant. "Don' know what it means, but they was sure you do."

Rufus blushed.

"We got a fresh pair of drawers, too, if ya ever need 'em," Lucinda added.

"I'll never live it down!"

"Don't ever think we'll let you," Harriman said.

The conversation covered the intervening years on into the afternoon until at last Rufus rose from his chair.

"I ought to be going. I don't want to get to my mother's too late. She gets tired." He walked around the table, stopping before each friend.

"You take care a yerself, Rufus Dewes, and come visit any time. Yer always welcome here. Cain't wait to have Jed read yer book to me," Lucinda said, giving him a hug.

"I'd be honored to read your book. Be good, Mr. Dewes."

"You too, Jed."

"I'll do it."

"I'll walk you out," Harriman said, leading Rufus onto the porch.

"Mr. Hickenlooper—er, Harriman, would you sign a book for me?"

"Only if you'll sign one for me."

"You're in luck. I just happen to have two with me."

They sat on a porch bench and exchanged autographs.

Rufus suddenly turned to Harriman. "One thing still kicks around in my head."

"Only one? You're a lucky man."

"Wasn't the reason for the bet that you find a place suitable for a monument? You never found one."

Harriman placed a hand on Rufus' shoulder and pointed to a bronze plaque embedded in a large boulder by the porch steps. The plaque read:

EDEN – A HOME FOR WAR ORPHANS
– MADE POSSIBLE BY THE SIXTH IOWA INFANTRY –
DEDICATED TO THOSE WHO DIED IN
THE WAR BETWEEN BROTHERS – MARCH 23, 1870

Rufus read the plaque. He read it again. He stuttered, choked up and tried to say something. Nothing came out. All he could do was wrap Harriman in a long embrace. Flustered, he tipped his hat, raised his autographed book and mounted his horse. As he rode off, he passed a covered wagon coming in the opposite direction. The wagon pulled up in front of the farmhouse.

Harriman went to the rear of the wagon, raised the flap and lowered the gate. "Come."

Several children peered out of the wagon. Harriman raised his arms and helped a boy down. Lucinda came onto the porch, calling out in her Southern drawl, "Welcome to Eden, children. Come inside." She took a child in each hand and led them into the house. The other children followed close behind them.

In a room across the house, away from the sounds of children laughing and dogs barking, stood another mantelpiece, much plainer than any in Walter Ridley's house. Sitting on it, in its own wood frame stretched on canvas, was a Stars and Stripes only a few had ever seen. It was certainly not the one Molly Hickenlooper had once promised her son.

For on it were a scrap from a Rebel Stars and Bars, speckled cloth from a rag doll dress, a shred of red bandanna and a button off an ex-slave's coat. Nestled in the center of these things was a small gold 'Co. D' from a Union Army forage cap. All had been carefully sewn into the spaces where she never finished.

*   *   *

"...It is rather for us to be dedicated here to the great task remaining before us – that from these honored dead we take increased devotion to that cause for which they gave the last full measure of devotion – that we here highly resolve that these dead shall not have died in vain, that this nation, under God, shall have a new birth of freedom..."

Abraham Lincoln
Gettysburg, Pennsylvania
November 19, 1863

AUTHOR'S NOTE

———————

I started writing this book fifteen years ago, in part spurred by a story I read in a book waiting for a flight home from South Carolina. It was about a man who made a one-man peace march right after the Civil War ended. At first I could not believe that such a story was true, given the hard feelings that ran so deep after the war.

The following year, I volunteered to work on a presidential campaign. Examining the 2000 electoral map, I sought another map, this one of the presidential election in 1860. If one lopped off every state west of the Mississippi, because that was basically what the map of our country looked like then (apologies to California), what these maps revealed was virtually the same story, namely that our nation was as divided now as it was seven hundred and fifty thousand dead and several million more wounded and homeless later.

The shooting has stopped, but the Civil War is not over. Its lessons and morals still call out to us, perhaps louder and more urgently than ever before. And its dead still ask us not just to remember them, but also to dedicate ourselves to find the ways to unify rather than tear apart this great country, one that has yet to recover from "Our War."